PRAISE FOR STEPHIE DAVIS AND *PUTTING BOYS ON THE LEDGE*!

"A fun read. *Putting Boys on The Ledge* is a good gift for the young adults in your life."

—*RT BOOKclub*

"Stephie Davis is a new voice to reckon with in the world of teen fiction. . . . A must have in any teenage girl's library."

—Erika Sorocco, teen correspondent
for *The Press-Enterprise*

"A joy to read, and I can't wait to read more from Stephie Davis. Her writing style is wonderful and so is this book."

—*Romance Reviews Today*

FIELD STUDY

"You ever slow danced with a guy before?"

I lifted my chin. "None of your business."

Theo shrugged, but there was that challenge thing blazing in his eyes again. "One dance."

"Why?"

"Education."

I almost laughed. "What kind of line is that?"

"I wouldn't waste a line on you."

"What does that mean?"

"You'd probably punch me in the stomach if I did."

I laughed. "Probably. You are a womanizing jerk."

"See? I knew it." He grabbed my hand and started walking backward, pulling me with him. "One dance. For research's sake."

Other SMOOCH books by Stephie Davis:
PUTTING BOYS ON THE LEDGE

Stephie Davis

STUDYING BOYS

SMOOCH NEW YORK

SMOOCH ®

August 2004

Published by

Dorchester Publishing Co., Inc.
200 Madison Avenue
New York, NY 10016

ISBN 0-8439-5382-9

Printed in the United States of America.

To Brooke Luallin,
an extremely courageous and special teenager.

STUDYING BOYS

Chapter One

There was no pizza.

As soon as I walked into the living room of my friend Blue Waller and saw her sitting on the couch with our other two friends, Natalie Page and Allie Morrison, and no pizza, I knew something was up.

You don't invite your friend to your house for pizza, and not have pizza, without something being up.

Not that I'd let them see I was surprised. I have a solid reputation going of being serious, together and always on top of things. It's taken a lot of work to build that reputation, and I wasn't going to start revealing other things now, like the fact that I kinda wanted to turn around and run out the door. You'd want to bolt too if you'd seen the look on Allie's face.

It was her "we're going to talk about boys" look.

Trust me, you didn't want to talk about boys with Allie. She's the queen when it comes to boys.

1

And I'm not.

I'm like your major underachiever in that department.

"Come on in, Frances." Blue smiled and patted the couch beside her.

"Where's the pizza?" I decided to hold firm in the doorway. Couldn't give up my avenue of escape.

"Oh, it'll be here eventually," Allie said vaguely.

Yeah, right.

This was not "Pizza Night." Something else was going on. Something that all three of them knew about and I didn't.

A clear indication that I wasn't going to like it.

"Frances. Sit." An order from Allie. What was up with that? We *never* order each other around.

"Why?" I folded my arms across my chest and tried to project my I'm-not-worried persona. It was Friday night. None of my friends ever do homework on a Friday night, so this definitely wasn't a study period. I, however, always get my homework done on Fridays. What if the house burned down over the weekend and I hadn't done my homework? I'd go to school unprepared, the teachers would flip, I'd lose my scholarship; then my parents would disown me and I'd have to turn to crime to support myself, and then I'd end up in prison and my entire career success would be defined by me walking down the side of the highway in a bright orange vest picking up trash with the rest of my prison work squad.

That sounds like a sucky way to live, so I get my homework done. And it's not because I'm a loser or anything like that. So what if I don't have a single guy friend, let alone boyfriend? So what if I have no social skills? It's not like I care.

Okay, maybe I care a little bit. Doesn't mean I'm going to sacrifice my entire future for some fun.

Blue stood up. "Frances, we're having an intervention."

"A what?"

"An intervention," Allie said. "Sit down."

I narrowed my eyes. "What's an intervention?" I was quite certain I didn't like the sound of it.

"It's what friends and family do for someone who has a problem and is in denial. We did it for my dad to get him to stop drinking," Allie said.

"But your dad took off after that and divorced your mom." Not that I wanted to make Allie feel bad, but it wasn't exactly a rousing endorsement of interventions.

"Ah, yes, well, we're pretty confident you won't divorce us," Allie said.

"Yes," Natalie chimed in. "You love us."

"For the moment, I love you." *Not so sure how I'll feel after this intervention thing.* "I don't drink, so what's my 'problem'?"

"Oh, for heaven's sake, Frances. Stop looking so worried."

Worried? I never look worried. I am way too together for that.

Blue slung her arm around my shoulder and practically forced me down into the chair next to the couch.

Yeesh. I felt like I was about to be interrogated for murder or something. My heart was actually racing. Racing! Was that a sign of weakness or what?

Blue returned to the couch next to Allie, while Natalie perched on the edge of her chair.

They all looked at me.

"What?" Oops. That sounded a little hostile and snappy. *Must stay calm.*

They glanced at each other, as if trying to decide who was going first; then finally Blue nodded. Apparently, she was in charge. She turned to me. "Frances. It's about Theo."

"Theo! Omigod! Is he okay? Did something happen? Did he get in a car accident?" Theo is Blue's older brother. He's a senior, and a total hottie. Of course, I've known him since I was three, and he only thinks of me as Blue's friend, but still. He's a stud. And now my heart was pounding so hard that I wouldn't have been surprised to see it burst out of my chest and race around the room screaming. "What happened to Theo?"

Blue looked a little smug. "Nothing. He's fine."

"Oh." Whew. Time to relax.

"But we need to discuss your crush on him."

"My *what?*"

"Your crush." Blue grinned. "Proven by you freaking out when you thought something had happened to him."

I was totally busted. I had no response.

Allie leaned forward. "Frances, we all love Theo, because we knew him when he was six and busted up his jaw crashing his bike. But now that he's a senior? He's a jerk when it comes to girls. You're way too sweet and nice for him."

"Theo isn't a jerk."

They all gave me the look.

"Okay, fine. So maybe he is a little bit." So what if he had ditched like eight girls in the past month alone? So what if he took them out for a drive and a little hanky panky and then never called them again? Maybe those girls just weren't right for him. Or maybe they were evil creatures from another planet trying to assassinate him, so he was picking them off one by one. . . .

Okay, so maybe I had a few issues when it came to Theo.

Maybe.

"Anyway," Blue continued, "we've decided that there's only one remedy to your obsession with Theo."

"I'm not obsessed with him." Obsessed was a little strong. So I thought he was cute. Big deal.

"Other boys," Allie announced.

I eyed her suspiciously. "What are you talking about?"

"The only way to effectively forget about Theo is to get some other interests in your life." She raised her voice over my protest. "And homework doesn't count."

"Why not?"

"Because homework sucks," Allie said. "Boys rock. No comparison."

Well, that was Allie for you. The world revolved around boys.

"So, we're giving you one week to get a new boyfriend, or to get involved in a coed activity, or else we're going to sit down with Theo and tell him that you like him. We'll make you sound like a stalker, so he'll feel awkward and uncomfortable around you. Then he'll avoid you all the time and you won't ever see him and it'll be impossible to continue to have your obsession with him if you never ever see him."

I swallowed. "You're going to tell Theo?"

Natalie shook her head. "Only if you don't get involved with a coed activity in seven days. One with boys."

"I know what coed means," I snapped. This was so unfair. Since when did they have the right to interfere in my life? Just because they'd been my best friends for my whole life didn't mean they had permission to destroy me! "But I go to an all-girls school. How am I supposed to find a coed activity?" Hah. Got 'em there.

Allie, who goes to school with me, shot me a smug little grin. Then she handed me a sheet of paper. "These are all the coed activities that our school does with Field School. You can pick one of these and get signed up, and then we won't talk to Theo. If you miss a meeting or drop out, then we'll tell Theo."

"Blackmail."

"Of course it is," Blue said. "That's what friends are for."

"I hate all of you."

Natalie's eyes widened. "Why do you hate us? We're just looking out for you. You take things way too seriously and we're worried you're missing out on all the fun of high school. You're halfway through your freshman year, and all you've done is study."

"So? I have good grades. I'm proud of them."

Allie rolled her eyes. "I've kissed twenty-two boys. I'm more proud of that."

"You're insane. You're all insane."

"I resent that," Blue said. Well, of course Blue could resent that. She had this super awesome senior boyfriend now. Life was perfect for her.

Natalie pointed to the list. "You have one week. Next Friday night, you have to bring us proof you've joined one of these clubs, or we're taking control of the situation."

"What about my parents?" Allie might not have parents who cared what she did, but Natalie and Blue would understand. "They'll never let me do anything that would take time away from my studies."

"Parents can be dealt with," Blue said. "You know that."

Said by the girl who had reasonable parents. Eccentric, but reasonable. "Mine don't think like normal people."

7

Natalie grinned. "There are four of us and only two of them. They have no chance."

And apparently, neither did I.

By Friday afternoon, I knew my life was over.

I was never going to see Theo again. The only guy I could ever love, and I'd never see him again after Friday. I hadn't joined any stupid club, and I wasn't going to. Which meant that my friends were going to tell Theo I was obsessed with him—which wasn't even true—and he'd run away screaming every time he saw me from now on. Which, of course, would only be when I went over to Blue's house for something, and then Theo would run upstairs and lock himself in his room to get away from me.

It was because I went to the wrong dumb school. If I went to the public school, then I'd see Theo in the halls and he'd get tired of running away from me, but no. My parents operated under the annoying delusion that in order for their oldest child to be the first one of the family to go to college, I had to go to an all-girls private school. On full scholarship, of course.

Which meant that once my friends told Theo I loved him, he'd avoid me and I'd never see him.

I hate my friends.

It was Friday afternoon at two o'clock and I hadn't joined any club. Hadn't met a single boy, except for the tattooed dude at the gas station who spit on our tires when my mom wasn't looking. Wonder if he'd qualify?

"Frances!"

I turned to find Allie jogging up behind me, wearing her girls-school clothes, which basically meant that she wasn't wearing a tight shirt and short skirt to show off her amazing bod. Why bother with that kind of outfit when you go to an all-girls school? No reason at all. "Hi, Allie. What's up?"

"So? What are you joining?"

"Nothing." I folded my arms across my chest and waited.

"Frances!"

"What?" I glared at her. "You really think my parents would let me join anything? I'm not allowed to do anything but homework and hang out with you guys, and that's only because I tell them we're doing homework when we're together."

"You *are* doing homework when we're with you. Didn't you read your history assignment during the movie the other night?"

"No." So I had the book open on my lap. So what? If the movie was boring, then I had something else to do.

"Come on, Frances. There has to be something you can do that your parents would approve of." Allie held out her hand and snapped her fingers. "Give me the list."

"Lost it."

"Fine." She grabbed my arm and dragged me over to a nearby bulletin board, which listed the times and

9

dates of meetings of some of the clubs. "Social Club. Join that one."

"Join a club whose function it is to set up social events with boys' schools? Yeah, I'm sure my parents would go for that one."

"I think it sounds fun."

"I'm sure you do." Okay, fine, I thought it sounded like fun too. I mean, how cool would it be to hang out with a bunch of guys and plan ways to have a good time? Not that I'd admit that to Allie or any of my friends. I had a reputation to uphold. Besides, it wasn't like I'd ever have the guts to show up at one of those meetings. No way. That was *so* not my style. I wasn't a joiner, and I sure as heck wasn't about to go throw myself in the middle of a group of kids who already knew each other, so they could point to me and say, "Look at the loser new kid. Who invited her?"

"How about this one? Physics Club? Even your parents wouldn't be able to say no." She peered closer. "Oh, sorry. Cancelled due to lack of participation."

"Allie, this is stupid. Let's go."

"No." Allie let out a cry of triumph and pulled a posting off the board. "Meeting is tonight at six o'clock. You have time to get there and still make the Friday-night deadline."

I took the notice and read it. "School newspaper?"

"Sure. You'd get to hang with the boys from Field School, but you'd also have to write lots of articles. Develop your writing and research skills. Learn how a paper runs. That's small-business skills right there. Your parents would be thrilled."

"Huh." I read the posting again. They were looking for staff writers. Maybe I could get assignments and not have to go to the meetings. Probably only the editors had to go to meetings. Not that I was *afraid* of going to meetings with a bunch of people I didn't know or anything. It was just that I had homework to do. "The meeting is actually not too far from my house."

"Walking distance," Allie agreed. "I think it's fate."

"I'll think about it." Who was I kidding? I wasn't going to go. I mean, it might be kinda cool to go and meet some other kids and stuff, but I wasn't the type to go out and socialize. I wouldn't know how to become a joiner even if I wanted to.

"I'll walk you." Allie tucked her arm through mine. "We'll swing by my house and get you some sexy clothes to wear and then I'll walk you over there."

"First of all, I'm not wearing sexy clothes. Second, why are you going to walk me?"

"Because if I don't, you'll wimp out."

"Hah. I'm totally not going to bag it." I had to find a way to ditch her before six o'clock so I could avoid going.

If I decided to skip it.

Not saying I was, but I needed my freedom to make a game-time decision.

"Nonsense. I'll be by your side every minute until I

drop you off." Allie gripped my arm tighter, like some psycho who was going to yank me into some dungeon and feed me beets for the rest my life.

Great.

I hate my friends. Have I mentioned that yet?

"So, here it is."

Natalie, Blue and Allie stopped in front of a small office building, while I lurked behind them.

"No one's there. Let's leave." I spun on my heel to make a break for freedom.

Allie grabbed my arm before I could sprint away. "There's a light on in the corner of the second floor. Didn't the directions say to take the elevator to the second floor?"

"I don't know." God! I couldn't do this! Walk into a room full of people who all knew each other and who would stare at me as if I were a freak? No way. How was this important in my life anyway? I got straight As. That was probably going to take care of me for college.

"I'm sure it said second floor." Allie started walking toward the building, her talons digging into my arm. I was going to have bruises after tonight. Bruises to remind me of the horror my life had become, thanks to my former friends.

"We'll just go with you to the elevators," Allie said.

Blue and Natalie fell in behind us, probably ready to grab me if I tried to run away. No problem. I'd get in the elevator and pretend I was going up to the meeting. I'd let the door shut, but not press any buttons. I'd hang out in the elevator for a few minutes, and once they'd gone back to Blue's house, I'd escape. Nothing like having a plan!

"Fine." I stopped struggling and started walking beside Allie. If I pretended to be willing to do it, they'd be more likely not to hang around and make sure I really went in.

"You know, Frances, I really think you should have worn some makeup," Allie said. "I mean, you have gorgeous dark eyelashes and stuff, but a little blush wouldn't hurt you."

"My parents don't let me wear makeup."

"You can take it off before you get home," Allie said. She glanced over her shoulder. "Either of you bring some mascara or blush?"

Blue laughed. "Are you kidding? We always use yours. You have the best stuff."

"Yeah, my mom spends a lot of money on her makeup," Allie agreed.

Makeup. I couldn't believe they were talking about makeup while I was having a complete breakdown.

Allie knocked on the door, and a security guard opened it. "Here for the paper?" he asked.

"Yep." Too bad I hadn't cut out Allie's tongue so she couldn't answer the question.

"Take the elevator to the second floor." The guard held the door open for us.

Jerk. Why couldn't he let the door slam shut in my face so I broke my nose and had to be rushed off to the hospital? Then I'd have to miss the meeting. It would totally be worth the swollen and bruised face.

But no, he had to stand there holding it open, as if he were doing us some favor.

As I said, jerk.

My palms were actually sweating. Nice.

Blue pushed the elevator button and we waited. I couldn't think of a single thing to say, other than to tell them that they were no longer my friends. Since that would clue them in that I was going to make a break for it after they left, I stayed strategically silent.

The elevator arrived . . . and everyone got in with me! This was all wrong! How was I supposed to escape if they came in with me? "What are you guys doing?"

"Riding up with you," Natalie said. "For support." She pushed floor number two, and the door started to close.

I stuck my foot in the door to keep it open. "You guys can't come up with me."

Natalie raised an eyebrow. "Why not?"

"Because I'll look like a loser if you guys ride up with me. It's like my mom dropping me off."

Natalie sort of frowned. Excellent.

Then Allie snorted and yanked me backward so my foot moved out of the doorway. "Don't be a dork. You'll look cool if you show up with friends."

14

The doors slid closed, and I felt like I was going to be sick.

Yes, that was the way to make a grand entrance in front of all those kids. Have the elevator doors open to reveal a vomiting loser being held up by her friends.

Have I mentioned that I truly despise my friends?

I watched the elevator click to two, wondering how old a person had to be to have a heart attack.

"Frances." Blue leaned over my shoulder.

"What?" I stared at the doors, willing them to get stuck closed.

"Allie made me try out for the play, and I was terrified."

"So?"

"So, it worked out. Have faith."

"Yeah, right." Okay, so maybe I wasn't projecting quite the totally-together attitude I'd been shooting for.

Too late now, as the doors opened to the second-floor lobby. Stupid doors. Hadn't I ordered them to stay closed?

But no. They'd opened, exposing me to a hallway full of kids. Boys. Girls. Chatting. Laughing. Arms around each other.

Then they all turned to look at me.

Oh, God.

Allie pushed me out into the hallway and the elevator door shut behind me.

I hate my friends.

Chapter Two

Everyone stared at me.

No one said anything.

Then everyone started chatting again and ignored me.

Which was good because I didn't have to talk to anyone.

Which was bad because I felt like a total loser, standing in front of the elevator in a roomful of kids with no one even acknowledging I was alive.

I should have worn Allie's revealing outfit and the makeup. Then at least *someone* might talk to me, even if it was only a toad who wanted to get a little action. At least then I'd look like I didn't have the plague.

I shoved my hands in the pockets of my jeans, backed up toward the wall, and just happened to press my elbow on the elevator button. I was going to slip out of there and forget it ever happened.

Elevator didn't come.

My friends were probably holding it downstairs.

They were so dead.

This *sucked*.

Someone whistled at the front of the room, and a guy walked in. He looked like he was pretty old, probably a teacher or something. Not from my school, because I knew all the teachers in my school. Maybe from Field School?

"Thanks for waiting! Let's go into the conference room and get started." He pointed toward a door to my right, and everyone started filing in there.

Stupid elevator still hadn't arrived.

No way was I going in that room.

Maybe no one would notice that I was in the lobby, and I could lurk out there until my former friends decided to release the elevator. Excellent plan.

"Hi, you're new." The advisor-teacher dude was standing in front of me. "I'm Mr. Walker. And you are?"

"Frances," I muttered.

"And you're from North Valley School for Girls?"

"Yeah." *Go away*.

"I'm a teacher at The Field School."

"I figured." So now what? Walk away? Tell him I'm in the wrong place?

17

"A little nervous, huh?"

"No." I lifted my chin and forced myself to look at him.

"Good. Come on in and we'll get you some work." Mr. Walker put his arm around my shoulders and propelled me into that stupid room with all those stupid kids. They were sprawled on chairs, and girls were giggling and making eyes at the boys and everyone was wearing makeup—well, the girls were. "Everyone, this is Frances. She's new, so be friendly."

Great. Does that make me sound like a loser or what? The teacher has to tell people to be nice to me. Excellent.

"Have a seat, Frances."

Where? All the seats were taken.

Oh, except the one right in the middle of the room. Front and center.

Yeah, right.

I walked over to the wall and sat on the floor, in the corner. I rested my hands on my thighs, but then realized they were shaking so badly that even people on the other side of the room would be able to see. So I shoved my hands under my legs instead. With any luck, I'd be invisible.

Mr. Walker started talking about the various articles that people had written, and then one boy who was pretty cute actually said that we needed to do something cool and new with our paper because people were getting bored with it.

So then everyone started brainstorming ideas and stuff and no one noticed me.

Good.

I liked it that way.

I certainly didn't care that I felt like a loser, and I wasn't going to wish people would talk to me. It wasn't as if I'd hoped that someone would think I actually mattered.

Okay, so I did wish that, sort of. I mean, how could I not? God, I felt like such an outcast. Was this really supposed to be fun? I mean, why would anyone subject themselves to this? I could be at home right now, finishing my homework and being all caught up. Or I could be at Theo's lacrosse game with Blue and her parents.

But no. I was stuck in some little office with a bunch of kids who didn't care if I existed. I was irrelevant.

Not a good feeling.

I took a deep breath and tried to think of something else, since I couldn't exactly sneak out without drawing attention to Loser Frances. I looked around the room and started counting how many kids I was being ignored by.

Once I looked around, I realized that I recognized some of the girls. Well, obviously I would, since they were all from my school. Great. So that meant on Monday, when I was walking down the hall, they'd point me out to their friends and say, "There's the weirdo girl who sat in the corner all night and didn't say anything."

"So, Frances? What do you think?"

I blinked, and realized Mr. Walker and the rest of the people in the room were all staring at me. "What?"

"Can you write that article?"

"Um . . ."

"You weren't listening?"

Okay, for the first time in my life, there was a teacher on my blacklist. Teachers loved me! So what was up with Mr. Walker completely humiliating me in front of everyone? The night was getting worse by the minute. "I was totally listening. Of course I'll write the article."

"Great. You'll want to set up The Homework Club by early next week, so you can have two months of sessions before the article is due. We'll want to publish it in the May issue."

The Homework Club? What was he talking about?

But he was already on another topic.

I spent the rest of the meeting hating myself for being stupid enough to actually say yes to the article. That meant I was going to have to come back, didn't it?

This *really* sucked.

I had to wait for thirty minutes after the meeting was dismissed for all the kids to stop talking to Mr. Walker so I could go up there and find out what The Homework Club was.

"Mr. Walker?"

"Yes, Frances?" He was picking up his papers and looked ready to leave.

"I'm really not sure what I'm supposed to be doing. I've never been on a paper or anything, and I didn't totally follow the discussion."

Mr. Walker paused and looked at me. "You want me to start at the top?"

Gah. He totally knew I hadn't been listening. "Yes, please."

"The group decided that the mission for this semester is to get the school administrations from both schools to agree to let seniors switch schools for their last semester."

Whoa. "You mean girls could go to Field School and boys could go to North Valley?"

"Yes."

"Wow. That'll never fly." North Valley was way too into female power and stuff to risk being contaminated by boys in the classroom. "Wait a sec. I'm not supposed to convince the schools to do that, am I?"

He smiled. "You're in charge of the first step."

"Which is?" I was really not liking the sound of this assignment.

"The Homework Club. You organize a study group of boys and girls that meets several times a week. They work together to quiz each other and do whatever it takes to bring everyone's grades up. If everyone's grades improve by the end of the semester, then it's the first step in providing proof that combining academics between the schools could work."

"No way." Was he kidding? "I'm supposed to organize that?"

"Yep. And write an article about the success of the program." He patted my shoulder like I was an obedient dog. "Everyone's counting on you. It's important that this project succeeds."

"I can't do it." I had homework to do. Obligations. No idea where to start. I didn't want the pressure or the responsibility or . . .

"You have to." Mr. Walker closed his briefcase. "Everyone else is already so busy with other projects, no one has time to take on this big of an assignment. You're the only one with an open schedule."

"But . . ."

Mr. Walker handed me a card. "Here's my e-mail address. Let me know how it goes and send me a note if you have any questions or want to run things by me. I can help you get a room at Field if you want to do it there."

"But . . ."

"Good luck, Frances. Keep in touch."

He ushered me toward the elevator, where a few kids were still milling around. One of them, a boy who had blond hair and was pretty tall and sort of cute, smiled at me. "Thanks for doing this, Frances. It would be so cool if we could get this to fly."

Whoa. He knew my name. He spoke to me as if I

were alive. I tried to smile back. "Yeah, sure. It'll be fun."

He nodded and got in the elevator.

I got in and so did Mr. Walker.

And I didn't feel like quite as much of a loser. I could ask that guy to come, right? And then I'd know one person.

The elevator opened on the first floor. "One more thing, Frances," Mr. Walker said.

"What?"

"In order to make this legit, you can't use kids from the newspaper, and the ones who join can't know the ultimate goal. It has to be successful on its own."

I looked at the boy again, all hope of getting to know him fading into oblivion. "Why?"

"Because if the kids know the purpose is to generate success for an exchange program, the administration could say they were on their best behavior and it wasn't indicative of the success of a coed program. So you need to make it work on its own."

So, I had to recruit boys and girls I didn't know? I had to get them to study? I was solely responsible for whether the administration from both schools agreed to an exchange program?

Excellent.

Not.

There was no way I could do this.

This was all the fault of my ex-friends.

My friends.

They'd *love* the idea. Their dear friend Frances having to recruit boys to study? They'd be all over it. I'd never have their support to bail.

But I had a secret weapon. My parents. They'd never let me do it.

Would they?

By the time I made my way home, it was almost ten o'clock. Mom and Dad were just sitting down to dinner, as usual. My dad never got home from work before nine. It gave my mom time to feed all my brothers and sisters and clear them out so she and Dad could have some quality time, whatever that was.

"Hi." I walked into the kitchen and sat down. I'd just tell them right now, have them ban me and then all would be good. It wouldn't be my fault, I would have fulfilled the requirements of the "Theo Deal" and my former friends wouldn't be able to tell him I liked him.

Seemed like quite a lot of torture to go through to return to status quo, but I wasn't going to worry about that. The important thing was to get my parents to say no.

"At the library tonight?" my dad asked. He was still wearing his blue work shirt, complete with grease spots. Ever since his garage had expanded the hours of the service department to nine o'clock, he never got home early enough to change before dinner.

Not that it mattered for him. If I, however, dared

grace the dinner table with a speck of dust, I'd be sent back to my room. Came with the burden of being the oldest child with parents who wanted to use me to break the cycle of generations of blue-collar workers.

"Um, no I wasn't at the library." I got up from the table and served myself some of the chili and grabbed some chips.

My mom looked startled. "You weren't studying?"

"No." Might as well raise the drama to make them more agitated so they'd forbid me from even thinking about The Homework Club, let alone running the stupid thing.

"Where were you? With Blue?."

"No." I sat back down at the table and started to eat.

"Frances!" my dad snapped.

I looked up. "What?"

"It's past ten. Where were you tonight?"

Parents. So predictable. "At some office building near here."

"What? Doing what?" My mom put down her spoon and glared at me. "You weren't vandalizing it, were you? Because there's no way we're going to tolerate you—"

"Mom! I wasn't vandalizing anything!" Geez. Talk about melodramatic. "I was at a meeting. I'm on the school newspaper."

Both my parents stared at me; then they erupted at the same time, shooting out question after question about the newspaper: who was running it, when it met, who was on it. You know, parent-type questions designed solely to find a reason to tell me I couldn't do it.

As I said, parents are so predictable.

I answered the questions to the best of my ability, and threw in some guesses when I didn't know. But it was when I started telling them about The Homework Club that everything really blew up.

"So, you're telling us that not only do you have to meet with an unruly group of kids who don't take work seriously, but you have to do it several times a week, plus you have to organize and recruit and *then* you have to write an article on it?" My mom's face was all twisted up. Big surprise. "So, when are you supposed to get your own homework done?"

I shrugged. "I don't know." Of course I knew. I'd get it done. No need to tell my parents that.

"No." My dad picked up his spoon and started eating again, ending the conversation.

"No? Just like that?" I asked.

"No," he repeated. "You're on scholarship, Frances. You can't afford to throw away your future on some . . . some . . ."

"Excuse for sex and drugs," my mom finished.

I choked on my milk. "Sex and drugs?"

"Of course. We weren't born yesterday. The Homework Club is just a cover for kids getting into sex and drugs. You can't do it. Earn your scholarship, get into college and be the first member of the Spinelli family to wear a suit to work." My mom pointed at my dinner. "Now eat."

I ate.

Victory!

Tomorrow I'd e-mail Mr. Walker and tell him I couldn't do it.

One question: Why didn't I feel excited right now? In fact, I felt totally bummed out.

What was up with that?

Sunday night, and I still hadn't e-mailed Mr. Walker.

What was wrong with me?

"I think it's because you actually want to do it," Blue said.

We were at Blue's house working on homework. Usually I'm done with mine by Sunday night, but not this weekend. Obviously, I didn't get any done on Friday, and I'd spent the weekend feeling sort of annoyed and I hadn't been able to concentrate. 'Course, that might've been because my five-year-old twin sisters had gotten the flu and had been throwing up all over the house and I'd had to clean everything up because my mom had to work overtime and my dad was at his security job. Then my eight-year-old sister, Dawn, had started a screaming fight with my ten-year-old brother, Kurt, and had scared the baby, who is only six months.

Sometimes being the oldest *sucks*.

My lack of concentration certainly hadn't been because I was upset that I couldn't join the newspaper and do The Homework Club thing.

"I agree with Blue," Natalie said. "Once your parents said you couldn't do it, you realized you wanted to."

"I don't want to." Did I? No. Ridiculous.

"Liar." Allie didn't even look up from painting her toenails metallic purple. "How could you not want to? Hang with boys and get to do homework at the same time? That's like your perfect night."

"It's not as if I *like* doing my homework all the time," I said. I mean, sure, I did it, but I wasn't a total loser. I didn't think it was the best thing ever. I had to do it, so I did it. Didn't mean I thought it was *fun*.

"Tell 'em you want to do it," Blue suggested. "It'll help your college application. They'll like that."

"I don't know," I said. "They said it was a front for sex and drugs."

My friends all laughed. They know my parents. "If my mom thought it was about sex and drugs, she'd probably invite herself along," Allie said.

"That's because your mom is cool," I said.

Allie tightened her lips and said nothing.

"So, what are you going to do?" Blue asked.

"They won't agree. I know they won't." It was partly my fault, of course. I'd pretty much presented it in a way to ensure they'd forbid me from participating. It wasn't as if I was going to get them to change their minds now.

"Does that mean you want to do it?"

Did I? "Um . . . I guess . . . maybe . . ." Who was I kidding? Of course I wanted to do it. I was also terrified and everything, but how could I not want to do it? Meet boys, become solely responsible for creating an exchange program between North Valley and Field, become a total diva that everyone knew and admired, and pad my college application while I was at it. Even I had to admit it was somewhat appealing.

"Then you'll have to lie."

We all stared at Allie. "You think I should lie? To my parents?"

"Of course. They won't agree, so how else are you going to do it?"

Whoa.

Lie to my parents.

"I can't lie to them."

Allie rolled her eyes. "Oh, come on, Frances. All kids lie to their parents about something."

I looked at Blue and Natalie. "Do you guys lie to your parents?"

Blue shrugged. "No, but I don't need to. I can talk them into anything."

Natalie pursed her lips. "Only about little things. Like that I got a bad grade on a quiz or something. And then, it's more like I just don't tell them, so it's not really lying, right?"

I looked at Allie. "Do you lie to your mom?"

Allie snorted and put the cap back on the nail polish. "Are you kidding? She could care less what I do. As long as she doesn't have to cancel one of her hot dates, she doesn't give a rip."

I sighed. "You're so lucky."

Allie grunted.

"Okay, so then what you have to do is not exactly lie," Natalie said.

"What do you mean?"

"When you're working on The Homework Club, just tell your parents you're doing homework. It'll be true, right?"

"Yeah, I guess."

Allie stopped blowing on her toenails. "I know. You can have The Homework Club at my house. My mom's never home anyway, and then if your parents ask you where you're going, you can say you're at my house. Which you will be. And then if they call you there, you'll be there. No lies at all. Simply some omissions."

Huh. No lies. "I don't know. It doesn't feel right."

Allie sighed. "Loosen up, Frances. After you finish and publish this great article and get all sorts of recognition, then your parents will realize what a good thing it was for you and they'll forgive you. Sometimes they don't know what's best for us."

Natalie nodded. "I agree. I think it sounds cool." She sighed. "I wish Blue and I could come, but it's only for kids from North Valley and Field, right?"

Blue looked up from her Algebra II book. "What? We can't go?"

Allie shook her head. "Don't be ridiculous." She turned to me. "Frances, first thing you need to do is e-mail this Mr. Walker and inform him that it isn't sufficient just to do it between two private schools. To truly test this project, you need to also include a coed public school."

"*What?* I haven't even decided whether I'm going to do it!"

"Of course you're going to do it. If you weren't, you would've e-mailed Mr. Walker already," Allie said. "Go e-mail him now about including Mapleville High."

"Now?" I swallowed.

"Yeah, do it now." Natalie sat up eagerly. "Come on. You can't leave Blue and me out of this."

"But . . ."

"Oh, come on, Frances," Blue said. "You and Allie will be spending so much time on this, we'll never get to see each other if we can't be part of the club. And maybe I'll even convince Colin to come and he can bring some of his friends."

Whoa. If Blue's boyfriend could come, then so could Theo. After all, Theo went to Mapleville High too. A glimmer of excitement raced through me. Maybe this wouldn't be so bad. Not bad at all.

Yeah, right. A chance to have Theo part of the club? I was all over it. "Okay, I'll do it."

Ten minutes later, courtesy of Blue's computer, I'd sent an e-mail off to Mr. Walker accepting the assignment and proposing the addition of Mapleville High.

The second I hit send, I felt this weird nervousness in my stomach. Excited, scared, and terrified of how I was going to deal with my parents on this one.

Too late now.

I was committed.

And I was psyched.

And afraid of my parents.

Not sure which was going to win out.

Chapter Three

It was Thursday night at five fifty-five.

The first meeting of The Homework Club was scheduled to start in exactly five minutes.

I hadn't told my parents.

And I was freaking.

Blue and Natalie were sitting on the stairs in Allie's front hall and they both looked annoyed. "I can't believe Mr. Walker didn't respond to your e-mail yet. Did you try again?" Blue asked. "Did you send him another e-mail asking him if you could invite Mapleville students?"

"I didn't e-mail him again, and no, he hasn't responded," I snapped. Why were they bugging me with that stuff? I had people due here in five minutes! I didn't have time to deal with my ex-friends!

"She just doesn't want us to come," Natalie said,

using her foot to poke me in the butt just as I was pulling out my room assignment list.

I spun around. "Stop it!" I screamed it, and my friends all stared at me, Allie on her way down the stairs in a micro-mini.

"Whoa. Frances. Chill," Allie said. "I've never seen you like this."

"Well, of course not. I've never had to arrange and host a stupid Homework Club before. If you guys are going to complain, I'm going to lock you in the basement until this is over." I glared at them. "Got it?"

They all shrugged and nodded and looked afraid of me. Good. That was exactly as it should be.

I took a deep breath and glanced around the front hall. "Okay, so we've got refreshments. Adequate lighting to read. Tables set up. Outlets available for laptops. Everyone studying science will be in the living room. English goes in the kitchen. Math in the den."

"Who's in the bedrooms?" Allie asked. "I'll join that group."

Natalie and Blue giggled while I yelled at Allie. "This isn't a social thing! You have to study! Go change your clothes! No boy is going to be thinking about homework if you wear that!"

"That's the point," Allie said. "Remember? The entire point of this was boys, if you recall."

Natalie wiggled her eyebrows and Blue grinned.

"Maybe it was about boys to *you*, but this is about the fact that I have an assignment to do!" Could I feel more guilty that my parents didn't know what I was doing? Guilty. Stressed. Surrounded by unsympathetic friends. It was a nightmare. "Okay, look, it's six o'clock now. You guys have to go upstairs." I tried to pull Blue and Natalie to their feet. "You haven't been approved by Mr. Walker so you can't come."

Blue looked offended. "You're kidding."

"How's Mr. Walker going to know if we're here?" Natalie narrowed her eyes. "You can't keep these private-school boys to yourself. We're worthy. I'm so sick of all the stupid boys on my track team. I need to meet some guys who don't smell."

"You're just annoyed because none of them asked you to the fall dance," Blue said. "You're friends with all these hot guys and none of them took you."

Natalie scowled. "I don't care about that. I don't want to date them anyway."

"Hey!" I waved my hands. "Go away!"

"Fine." Blue stood up. "Let's go upstairs and call Colin. Maybe we can go out with him and his friends."

"What?" They were going to go out without me? That wasn't fair.

Blue flipped a look over her shoulder as she and Natalie walked up the stairs. "If you'd gotten permission for Mapleville High to come, then maybe Colin would've brought all his friends here."

I was about to die from stress and they were trying

to make me feel worse? What kind of friends were they?

Allie put her arm over my shoulder. "Don't worry about them, Frances. They'll raid my mom's makeup cabinet and be fine." She glanced at her watch. "Five minutes after. People should be arriving any minute. Let's go get the food ready."

"You get the food. I'll review the rotation schedule."

Allie shook her head. "You're way too serious. No one's going to come back if you don't lighten up."

"Said by the woman who doesn't have to write an article that both schools are relying on to change policy."

"Better you than me." Allie hiked up her skirt still farther. "You really should borrow some of my clothes sometimes. Those baggy clothes really don't do you any justice."

"Allie!"

"Fine. I'll go get the food. Relax."

Phew.

Okay.

This was under control.

I was ready for everyone to arrive.

My first guest arrived at precisely ten minutes after six. I opened the door to find a guy about as tall as me, and about as skinny as Natalie, which meant he was basically all skin and bones. "Hi."

He shifted on the step and fixed his glasses. "So, is this The Homework Club?"

"Yeah. Come on in." I stepped back and waved him inside.

I was pleased to see his backpack was full of books and he was carrying two others in his arm. "I'm Frances Spinelli."

"George. George Moon." He glanced around. "Am I the first one here?"

"Yep." I peered past him into the street, but no one was there. "Did you walk?"

"My mom dropped me off. She'll be back in an hour. I didn't know how long it would go, and I didn't know if it would be productive, so I'm only going to stay for a short time."

"Don't worry. We'll be productive. As soon as the others arrive, we can get started. . . ."

George looked concerned, with his black-rimmed glasses and red hair that didn't quite lie flat. "Why can't we start now?"

"Oh. I . . . um . . ."

Allie walked around the corner. "Go ahead and start studying, Frances. I'll guard the door and direct people."

"Well, okay." I hated to relinquish control, but George did have a point. We might as well get started. I handed Allie the chart. "Make sure you send people to the right rooms."

She rolled her eyes. "I think I can handle it."

"Can we get started?" George said. "I only have fifty-five minutes now."

"Right." I grabbed my book bag. "What do you want to work on?"

He eyed me. "You and I are going to study together?"

Did he see anyone else, besides my friend in the spiked heels? "Yeah."

"You're a freshman?"

"Uh huh."

He nodded. "Me too. Want to do some biology?"

"Sure." I thought about the rotation. "So, we'll go in the living room. Remember, Allie, science goes in the living room."

"Right, Chief."

I took George into the living room and we set up our stuff. Our classes were on different topics, but I'd already covered what he was working on, so we sorta chatted about the life cycle of plants and compared notes.

George was actually pretty smart, and I could tell he was really into the discussion. Which was cool. See? This concept could work.

About five minutes later, the doorbell rang again. "I'll get it!" I yelled.

Way cool. The crowds were coming now!

I abandoned George in the middle of explaining a diagram in his book and rushed to the front door. Allie had already opened it, and she flipped me a look. "It's George's mom."

"Why?"

Allie raised an eyebrow. "It's been an hour."

"No way." I looked at my watch. An hour and five minutes actually. Cool. Studying flew by. This rocked.

George appeared next to me with his bag all packed up. "So, um, Frances. It was a good night. If you have it again, let me know." He handed me a piece of paper with his e-mail address. "And if you ever want to study with me again, e-mail me." He grinned, his braces catching the light of the hall chandelier. "Seriously."

"I had fun too." I took the paper. "I'll definitely e-mail you."

He sort of ducked his head. "And I'll try to get some of my friends to come next time. If you think there will be more girls here, I mean."

"More girls?" Oh my God. *No one else had come.* I'd been so caught up in studying with George, I hadn't even thought about it.

He turned red. "Not that there's anything wrong with you. Like I said, I'll study with you anytime. I just meant that my friends might not come if there aren't more people. Let me know, you know?"

He sort of waved and then ducked out the front door, to where his mom was already back in the car waiting for him.

Allie gave a friendly wave, then pushed the door shut. "We have *got* to talk. Natalie! Blue! Get down here!"

"So, um, where exactly did you put the signs?" Blue asked.

I grabbed another piece of pizza and shoved it in my mouth. "Everywhere. I put them on every bulletin board at school."

"And I went over to Field and put 'em up there too." Allie shook her head. "I totally timed it wrong. It was after school so there were no boys around. What's the point in going to Field if you don't get to talk to boys?"

"And I put a little blurb thing in the newsletter for both schools," I said.

Unbelievable. Only one person had shown up. One!

Blue picked some pepperoni off the pizza and dropped it into her mouth. "My parents would kill me if they knew I was eating meat."

"And mine would kill me if they knew I tried to have a Homework Club meeting tonight." So, lying to my parents, stressing all week, it had all been for nothing. Total and utter failure. "I suck."

"Hey." Natalie threw a pillow at me. "You're the practical one. The planner. If this was one of us, you'd be all over us with theories and plans about how to fix this situation. So start talking."

"I have no idea."

Natalie rolled her eyes. "Frances! Think!"

"I have a thought," Blue said. "When I told Colin about it, he said it sounded boring. Said no one in their right mind would go to anything called The Homework Club."

"I second that," Allie said. "The only reason I was here was for the boys."

"But it's not a social thing," I said. "The whole point is to do homework."

"Wake up, Frances. You're the only one who would think homework is fun," Blue said.

"And George Moon," Allie said. "I think he's your perfect match, Frances."

"Well, he was cute." And he studied hard.

"Yeah, in a dorky sort of way," Allie said. "You two should have seen him. I think he might have been even more serious than Frances."

. While my friends made fun of poor George, I chewed my pizza and started thinking about how I was going to tell Mr. Walker I was a total failure.

"You're giving up?"

I looked at Allie, who was staring at me in dismay. I guess when you've been friends since you were three, you can't hide your thoughts. "Yeah, so?"

"You can't give up." Allie set her pizza down. "It's simple. All you have to do is get Mr. Walker to let you have Mapleville High involved. And then we can get Colin to bring hot senior guys and my sister will bring some of her friends, and then we'll be the coolest thing around, and we'll be the only freshmen who get to hang with seniors."

"Yeah! And then we can come," Natalie said. "It's really the only way, you know. None of us know anyone influential at Field School to get those boys to come."

"George said he'd bring more friends," I said.

Allie raised an eyebrow. "Only if you got more girls. And what girls are going to come if the only boys are freshman geeks like George?"

"Hey! He was nice."

"But is he the kind of guy who's going to draw a crowd?"

Maybe not.

Definitely not.

I was doomed.

I could give up and admit failure.

But my stupid parents never let me give up on anything. Said I'd never go to college if I started having that attitude.

Of course, their advice would probably be different if they knew it was The Homework Club.

But . . . what if I could make this work? I mean, how cool would that be? I'd be a legend at North Valley forever, as the girl who got the exchange program started.

Think what that could do for a college resume.

And maybe . . . just maybe . . . if kids from Mapleville could participate, then maybe Theo would come. . . .

"All right, I'll e-mail Mr. Walker."

And I had to do something about my parents.

* * *

STUDYING BOYS

The e-mail from Mr. Walker was on my computer when I got home from school on Monday.

> *Dear Frances,*
> *I think your proposal to expand The Homework Club to Mapleville High has merit. You may go ahead and invite a select few students to attend. I will look forward to seeing the article in about seven weeks and I expect regular updates in the meantime.*
>
> *Mr. Walker*

Phew.

Deep breath.

I immediately e-mailed Allie to go talk to her sister, and then I decided to go over to Blue's house to discuss her inviting Colin. You know, because then maybe Theo would overhear us talking and want to come too.

I walked into Blue's house right when her family was sitting down to dinner. A family dinner. With her parents, Blue, her little sister Marissa . . . and Theo.

Theo's dark hair was sort of messed up, and it was getting long. He was wearing a torn black T-shirt and looked wicked hot.

"Frances! We didn't know you were coming! Please come join us." Blue's mom jumped up from the table and pulled up a chair.

OMG. She was putting me next to Theo!

He didn't even glance at me, just kept eating his tofu lasagna. I knew it was tofu even without looking at it. Blue's mom would never serve real meat.

"So, um, hi, everyone," I said, sneaking a peek at Theo, who was still eating.

Marissa grinned at me and sucked a noodle off her plate. While her mom was scolding her for poor manners, I looked at Blue, who was across from me. I tried not to notice Theo's arm was only about six inches from mine. "So, Blue, Mr. Walker e-mailed me back. He said it was cool to ask some kids from Mapleville."

She let out a whoop and held her arms over her head in a sign of victory that caught the attention of everyone at the table. Even Theo was looking at her.

"Blue? You have something to share with the rest of the family?" her dad asked. There were no secrets in Blue's family. Her parents were into the family bonding thing. As Blue's friend since we were babies, I also fell under the Waller Family Rules. No secrets.

"Yeah." Blue quickly launched into a description of The Homework Club, thankfully leaving out the mortifying details of the terrible first meeting. "So, I'm going to call Colin and tell him to come."

Theo snorted. "To a Homework Club? Sorry Blue, the dude may be whipped but there's no way he's going to join anything called The Homework Club. And there's no way he's going to get his friends to go."

I felt myself shrink in my chair.

"Nonsense, Theo, it's a marvelous idea," Mrs. Waller said. "Frances, you girls can have it here if you want. I'll make some desserts and take care of all the food."

I exchanged nervous glances with Blue. Her mom's desserts would end all chances of a successful event. The health food thing didn't mesh well with food that tasted good. Especially when it came to dessert. "Um, that's okay, Mrs. Waller. We're doing it at Allie's house."

"Allie's? But isn't her mom always gone?"

"Yeah." I glanced at Blue, who shrugged.

"So, how are you going to keep all the kids under control if there aren't parents around?" Mrs. Waller asked.

"That's not what this is like," I said. "It's just about homework."

"As I said, sounds fun," Theo said. "Sure wish I could go."

Mr. Waller looked at Theo. "Why don't you go? Then you could help the girls keep everyone in line."

My stomach immediately did a triple flip and I felt like I was going to fall off my chair.

Theo laughed. "Yeah, Dad, I'll be all over that. Baby-sitting my sister's friends? Sorry, but that's not going to happen."

Baby-sitting? He thought of me as someone who needed baby-sitting?

"Oh, now look, Theo, you've made Frances cry," Mrs. Waller said."

What? I wasn't crying! How could she say that? There weren't even tears in my eyes! Yeah, sure, I was totally humiliated and wanted to crawl under my chair, but I absolutely was *not* crying!

Theo shot me a look. "Sorry, Frances. Didn't mean it like that."

OMG. Could this get any more embarrassing? "I'm not crying!"

Mrs. Waller patted my hand. "It's okay, Frances. I can tell you want to. You don't need to hide anything from us."

"Don't be ridiculous," Blue scoffed. "Theo could never make Frances cry. She's just upset because one of her sisters is very sick and she's worried about her."

I have the best friend on the planet.

Of course, then I had to launch into a detailed story about how my younger sister, Dawn, was sick, and I felt really bad about lying, but it wasn't my fault. Blue had brought it up and I was just protecting *her* from being exposed as a liar. So, since I was doing it to help Blue, then there was nothing wrong with it, right?

Right.

First, lying to my parents about The Homework Club.

Second, lying to Blue's parents about Dawn being sick.

What was happening to me?

Forty-five minutes later, Blue hung up the phone after talking with her boyfriend, Colin. Colin was a senior at

Mapleville High, and he was totally hot and he adored Blue. He would *so* help us.

Blue shook her head. "He says he'll come, but he's not bringing any friends."

"What? Why not?"

She grimaced. "He said he can't ask his friends to come."

"But why?"

"Because . . . well . . . it's a Homework Club. It's not very cool."

"But if they come, then they'll make it cool." How could he be doing this? "I thought he'd do anything for you."

Blue laughed. "Well, I think I've found out his limit."

I sat down on the bed. "Well, this sucks. I mean, totally."

"Let's call Allie. See what her sister said." Blue put her phone on speaker and dialed Allie, who answered on the first ring. "Allie, it's Blue and Frances. What did Louisa say?"

"She laughed in my face and told me there was no way on this planet she'd ever be associated with a homework anything." Allie sounded morose. "I even told her Colin was going to come, and she said that didn't matter because Colin has a girlfriend already so he's hardly eligible meat."

I flopped back on the bed and groaned.

"Yeah, Colin won't bring his friends either," Blue said.

Allie swore. "Well, what now? We've used all our connections."

This was my payback for lying to my parents. They'd always told me that dishonesty didn't pay, and now I was suffering because of it.

"There's one more person with the social power to make this thing fly," Blue said.

"Who?" Allie asked.

I sat up. "Yeah, who?"

Blue looked at me. "Theo."

My heart literally stopped in my chest and Allie howled in protest. "Blue! Are you kidding? The entire point of this exercise was to get Frances to think about anything *other* than Theo!"

"You have any other ideas?" Blue asked, still looking at me.

Oh, God. I felt like I was going to faint.

Allie was silent, and the only sound I could hear was my heart whooshing in my ears.

"You better call Natalie," Allie said finally.

"Fine." Blue grabbed her cell phone and dialed Natalie, quickly explaining the situation while Allie made disapproving noises and I tried to keep from throwing up. When Blue finished, she listened to Natalie for a sec, then nodded. "Natalie agrees with Allie that bringing in Theo would be detrimental to Frances's emotional well-being. But she also agrees that there's no other option. She thinks we should go for it, and just make sure that George Moon keeps coming so Frances can date him."

"Ohhh . . . that's a good idea. Forgot about George," Allie said. "You liked George, didn't you, Frances?"

"Actually, yeah, I did." I could actually speak to him coherently and not pass out when I was in his presence, which was always a good thing. "He'll come back."

"Then it's settled," Allie said. "Frances, go talk to Theo, and do it where Blue's parents can overhear so they intervene and make him go. We really can't afford for him to back out too. He's our only chance."

"Whoa." My tongue felt so big and thick I was surprised I could speak. "*I* have to talk to Theo?"

"Of course you do. It's your event, isn't it? We're behind the scenes," Allie said.

Blue held out the phone. "Natalie wants to talk to you."

I took the phone. "Nat?"

"If you can get Theo and his friends to go, I think I'll be able to get some of the kids on my track team to come. Boys and girls. Theo's like the ultimate athlete and people will go where he goes. So go talk to him, and don't think of him as a guy you have a crush on. Just think of him as your brother, which he practically is anyway."

I handed the phone back to Blue without responding. My throat was so tight there was no way I could talk.

"Frances! Blue! It's time for dessert!" Mrs. Waller yelled up the stairs, and I jumped.

"We'll talk to Theo now, at the dinner table. My parents will be there," Blue said.

Oh, like Theo would dig being forced to hang with me by his parents. That was *not* the way to get his attention, or at least the type of attention I wanted.

"Good. And then Frances has to e-mail George Moon. That's the relationship we need to cultivate," Allie said. "Frances? Did you hear me? You're going to e-mail George tonight, right?"

"Yeah." Gah. Did my voice sound strangled or what?

Blue hung up her cell phone. "Nat says good luck."

"Good luck from me too. Call when you finish and let me know how it went." Allie disconnected and Blue hung up that phone too.

And then she looked at me. "You don't look so good."

"I think I'm going to be sick. Maybe we should do this another night."

"Give me a break, Frances. He's my obnoxious brother. I don't know why you have this thing about him." Blue stood up and dragged me to my feet. "Let's go. I'll back you up, but you have to start."

Oh, God.

I was never going to be able to do this.

But I had to. This was my big chance to get Theo to notice me. If he saw how smart I was, then maybe he'd realize I wasn't some kid who needed baby-sitting.

Yeah, that's right. If I was running this whole thing, then he'd realize I was an adult and worthy of him.

So, all I needed to do was go down there, act totally cool, and ask him to come to The Homework Club and bring all his friends.

No problem.

As long as I didn't pass out on the way down there.

Chapter Four

I made it down the stairs without falling and breaking my neck.

Unfortunately.

Followed Blue into the dining room.

Sat down next to Theo.

Stared at my strange-looking pastry thing and wished I was anywhere but there.

The conversation started with a casual discussion of Theo's lacrosse team and how they were the favorites to win the state champs even though it was only the end of March.

Then Blue kicked me under the table so hard I choked on my dessert. Spit it all over my plate, in fact. A little bit of my chewed-up pastry landed on the edge of Theo's plate.

Great. Nothing like wanting to die.

He was staring at my regurgitated dessert like it was going to jump off the plate and attack him.

"Sorry," I muttered, using my napkin to clean up the mess.

No way could I ask him now. No way!

"Frances," Blue said, with a tone that said she was going to bring it up if I didn't.

I glared at Blue. "Shut up."

"Now, Frances, you know we don't allow that kind of talk in this house," Blue's mom said.

Yeah, yeah. But this was a special circumstance. I had to stop my friend from forcing the ultimate humiliation on me.

Blue eyed me for a second, and I realized she wasn't going to be stopped. I hadn't even gotten my chair pushed back to bolt out of the room before she said, "Theo. Frances has something she needs to ask you."

The entire table turned to look at me. Theo included. With his bright blue eyes, black hair and ratty T-shirt. "What do you need, Frances?"

"Nothing. I have to leave. I have homework to do."

"She wants you to join The Homework Club," Blue said calmly, as if she weren't destroying my world.

Theo laughed. Actually, he snorted. With derision. He snorted with derision at the thought of joining my Homework Club.

Excellent. My humiliation was complete.

"I think that's a great idea," Mrs. Waller said, to

which Theo promptly snorted again and drank his purified water.

No reply necessary, apparently.

"Why do you want Theo to join?" Mr. Waller asked me. "He's not exactly studious." He shot Theo a sharp look that told him exactly what he thought of Theo's study habits.

Blue folded her arms across her chest and blinked at me.

She wasn't going to bail me out.

I hate you, I mouthed to her. She shrugged and smiled.

"Frances? Why do you want Theo to help?"

I stole a look to my right, and Theo had stopped eating and was watching me. OMG. Like I'm supposed to be able to talk with him watching me?

Look at Mr. Waller. Right. I turned away from Theo and focused on his dad. "We're not really having a lot of success with people attending The Homework Club." I rushed on before Theo could make another derogatory remark about it. "So we need someone popular to come. Someone who other kids follow. Someone who will make The Homework Club cool."

Theo eyed Blue. "Colin refused, huh?"

"He said he'd come, but no friends."

"What about Louisa?" Theo asked.

"She said no," I said. "But I'm sure she'd come if you came." Yuck. How pathetic did that sound? Begging. Telling Theo how everyone did whatever he wanted. I shouldn't be feeding his ego! Wasn't that against the whole Ledge thing that Allie was always talking about?

Oh, who was I kidding?

I was desperate.

I had no social skills.

Theo already thought of me as someone who needed baby-sitting.

Any chance for pride was already long gone. I was long past pathetic. All I had left was the chance to succeed at The Homework Club, because any chance to win Theo was completely destroyed. So I turned to Theo and faced him straight up. "Listen, Theo. I need this to be successful because I have to write an article on it. I don't know anyone else who can help. I need you to come and bring friends. Make it cool. Make it work."

Okay, so it sounded like I couldn't do it without him. Well, it was true, wasn't it? But man, it really hit my gut to have to admit I needed him. A guy! Where was all the girl power my stupid all-girls school always preached? Nowhere!

Theo gave me sort of a half smile. "Sorry, Frances. I can't help you out."

At least he didn't snort at me. So I could crawl back into my shell with some semblance of pride.

"Theo." Uh oh. Dad Waller looked serious.

Theo's grin faded at he looked at his dad. "What?"

"Help out the girls."

"Dad! I have practice!"

"I'm sure they'll schedule around it."

"But it's a Homework Club. Homework!"

"Exactly. Your grades need it and you need to help out the girls. It's about family, Theo."

Yeah, that's exactly what I wanted, for Theo to think of me as *family*. What kind of lustful dreams would he have about *family?*

Theo put his fork down and glared at his dad. "I'm not going to a Homework Club, and I'm not dragging my friends."

"Then no lacrosse."

Oh, wow. This wasn't good. Theo was going to *hate* me.

Theo glanced at his mom, who nodded. Of course she'd nod. Blue's parents always stood by each other.

Then he glared at Blue.

Didn't even look at me.

He just got up from the table and left.

Okay, then. That went well. Theo would be banging down my door with declarations of love in no time. Either that or he'd be coming after me with a pickaxe.

Blue's dad grinned at me, looking very pleased with himself. "There you go. Theo's on board. Just give him the time and date and how many friends you want, and he'll be there."

Excellent.

Not.

* * *

Monday night. Ten past seven. At Allie's house. Waiting for The Homework Club attendees, who were already ten minutes late.

I looked at my friends, who were munching popcorn and watching television. How could they be so relaxed? Didn't they realize what a big deal this was?

We'd started an hour later so Theo could come after practice. With his friends.

But it was ten minutes after with no Theo.

Not even George had come.

I walked into the living room and stood in the doorway. "This isn't working."

Allie looked up. "They'll come. Boys like Theo need to be fashionably late."

"Late? For a Homework Club?" That made no sense. This wasn't a party. This was like study hall.

"Chill, Frances," Allie said. "Have some popcorn."

"No."

I walked back to the front of the house, and tried not to think about lying to my parents tonight. I'd told them Allie and I were doing a research project together on the Bolshevik Revolution, so we'd be working together a lot over the next two months.

Liar!! I was a liar!!

I felt sick.

Then the doorbell rang.

And I felt more sick.

But I walked over to it and opened it. "Hi George."

George gave me a shy sort of smile and held out a

plate of brownies. "My mom thought you might want food for tonight."

"Thanks." I glanced past George. Just his mom waving at me from the front of her station wagon. I waved back, then shut the door.

"So, just you and me?" George looked sort of pleased. "Into the living room?"

"Um, no. My friends are watching television. How about we go to the kitchen and do math, or the den and do English?"

"How about math?"

"Sounds good." I sighed and led the way back to the kitchen, walking past the television set. "Maybe you guys should be studying."

"Not without the boys," Allie said.

I glanced at Blue. "Where's Colin? I thought he was coming tonight."

"He'll be here."

Right. The fashionably late thing again. What was up with boys? Why'd they have to be late for everything? What was wrong with being on time?

At least George was here, with his red hair and glasses. George was my type.

We sat down at the kitchen table and pulled out our books, and then I learned that the right boy could make math interesting. He was funny, thought up cool examples for explaining things, and he totally loved talking math. How could I not have fun doing math when I was laughing the whole time? Plus I was learning! How awesome was that? It was so great to finally meet someone who was as dedicated to homework as I was. He didn't make me feel strange for being into school because he felt the same way! Made me realize how much I missed that kind of respect from everyone else in my life—except of course my parents, who were psycho, so they didn't count.

About twenty minutes later, the doorbell rang. George's mom already?

"I'll get it," Blue shouted.

Right. Colin. As if he'd do any studying. He'd be mooning over Blue.

This Homework Club was a total and utter failure.

For everyone else. For me, at least, I had a study partner, right? So it wasn't a total loss?

I heard a loud crash from the front of the house, and then a bunch of shouting and then loud music started cranking. What was going on?

"Hang on a sec." I barely looked at George before I jumped up and ran to the front of the house, slamming to a stop as soon as I rounded the corner.

There had to have been at least forty kids there. Boys, girls, all of them older. I didn't know anyone.

Then I saw Theo in the corner. Theo! He'd come through! I would love him forever.

Then he turned around and I saw he'd been leaning

over the CD player. He was the one cranking out the music?

"Who wants to dance?" he shouted.

At least six giggly girls in obscenely tight outfits rushed over to his side, grabbing his arms and hands to drag him into the middle of the room, where they all started dancing around him.

You have *got* to be kidding.

Then more boys and girls joined in, and I could actually feel the floor shaking.

I heard the sound of liquid exploding, and turned to my right in time to see soda spray all over some guy, while a girl I didn't know opened one of six boxes of pizza and started handing out food.

And in the corner a couple was going at it in the big armchair.

I didn't even know how to respond.

I felt a tap on my shoulder and I spun around. "What?"

It was George. "What's going on?"

"I have no idea." *Except that Theo is a total scum who is going to pay*.

"I can't study with this music."

"Me neither." And neither could all these other kids.

"Who are all these people?" George sounded more than a little put out, and I couldn't blame him. He'd come to study and gotten some wild party.

"I don't know."

There was Allie, draped over some guy on the "dance floor." Blue was snuggled on the couch with Colin, cheering Allie on, and Natalie was sitting next to Blue, looking a little uncomfortable.

"Fix this, or I'm leaving," George said.

Fix it? How was I supposed to fix it? March up to a bunch of seniors and tell them to shut up? I was a freshman. They'd never listen to me. Ever. "You fix it," I snapped.

George looked at me. "I'm not the one in charge."

Yeah, right. He was just as afraid of all of them as I was.

But I had to do something. This was worse than having no one. This was proving that The Homework Club would never work, which meant that the proposal to comingle the two schools wouldn't pass, and it would all be my fault.

My heart was racing and the music was pounding in my ears. Theo was slow dancing with some girl who had her hands in the back pockets of his jeans. Disgusting. Slut. What kind of girl would do that?

Not that I cared who Theo was with. At least, not at the moment. My life was falling apart.

"I'm calling my mom." George walked back into the kitchen, leaving me with a bunch of gyrating seniors, blasting music and food. And I didn't see one textbook anywhere.

That was it. I was getting help.

I made my way across the room, dodging bodies

and shrieking girls, and stopped in front of Colin, Blue and Natalie. "You guys have to help me!"

Natalie's eyes widened. "How?"

"Make them study." I looked at Colin. Blue and Natalie would have no more influence than I did. Only a peer would have any influence over these seniors. "Colin, please."

He looked apologetic. "Sorry, Frances. These aren't my friends. They aren't going to listen to me."

"Of course they will! You're cool!"

He looked a little embarrassed. At least there was one guy who didn't thrive on being adored. "They're Theo's friends."

"Then talk to Theo!"

Colin eyed me. "Why don't you talk to him?"

I turned and looked at Theo, who now had two girls hanging on him while they danced. Yeah, *right*. As if there was any chance I was walking up there. "Please, Colin. *Please.*"

Blue elbowed him. "Just go talk to him."

Colin rolled his eyes, but he got to his feet and walked over to Theo. I collapsed next to Blue. "You have a good boyfriend."

Blue just smiled and looked happy. Great. I was so pleased for her. Well, I was sort of happy for her. But also it was a pain. She was different than the rest of us, with her boyfriend. And maybe I was a little jealous. Not a lot. But maybe a little. Not that I wanted Colin, but would it be so bad to have a nice guy actually think I was worth something and actually do favors for me?

Colin caught Theo's arm. Just reached between those squirming female bodies and grabbed him. Yeah, as if I could've done that.

Theo disentangled himself from the girls and stepped aside, his head bent in conversation with Colin. How cute did he look, listening to Colin? It was obvious he respected Colin, with the way he nodded. It wasn't the kind of look he ever gave me. My look was more along the lines of, "Shouldn't you be in bed by now? It's past seven o'clock."

Colin nodded, Theo slapped him on the back and they parted ways. Theo went back to his girls and Colin walked over to us. "Sorry, Frances. He's not interested."

"In what?"

"Studying." Colin sat down next to me, since I'd taken his spot next to Blue. "He said he was forced to attend but that doesn't mean he has to work."

I narrowed my eyes and tried to incinerate Theo with my gaze. No such luck. "Is that really what he said?"

"Yeah. He said he promised his friends a fun party with no parents and that's what he's going to give them."

What a total jerk. I watched a girl grab Theo's butt, and I wanted to run over and rip all her stupid blond hair out. I mean, I wanted to go over and staple Theo to the wall so I could scream at him for an hour about what a selfish ingrate he was.

"Sorry," Colin said. "I tried."

"It's okay." Blue reached around me and patted him on the shoulder. "Thanks for going over there. Theo's kind of an idiot, so don't worry about it."

Yuck. I wasn't in the mood to be in the middle of some sort of mushy love stuff.

I stood up and stalked across the dance floor, bumping into three flailing couples and shooting them all evil looks. Not that they cared or noticed. Yes, I felt invisible.

George was just opening the front door when I passed through the front hall. "You're leaving?"

"Yeah." He looked around. "This isn't my scene."

"Mine either."

He sort of eyed me. "Why don't you come with me? My mom can drop us off at the library and then she can give you a ride home."

Oh, wow. Was he like asking me out on a date? Suddenly, I had goose bumps going all down my arms and my brain stopped.

"Frances?"

I had no idea what to say. I mean, this was my first date invitation ever. I couldn't go on it without preparation! Not that George was this super cool senior or anything, but he was a guy!

"I really should stay. I'm supposed to be running this thing."

"Oh, right. Sure. No problem."

At that moment, some girl came running through

the front hall, shrieking about something. She slammed into me, apologized, and then kept on going into the other room.

Who was I kidding? This sucked.

"Let me get my books."

I couldn't sleep.

It was three in the morning, and I still hadn't slept.

I'd bailed from The Homework Club seven and a half hours ago, had a great study session with George, gotten inside with my parents totally oblivious, snagged some chocolate cake and I was still so angry at Theo I felt like I was going to explode.

How dare he ruin everything for me? Didn't he care how important this was to me? And not just to me, to the kids at both schools. So many people were counting on this, even if they didn't know it, and he'd waltzed in there and made it a total disaster.

I couldn't even think of enough bad words to call him.

He was so not worthy of my love.

He wasn't even worthy of my hatred.

Or perhaps he was.

Yes, he definitely was.

I stared at the ceiling and imagined locking Theo in my basement and beating him with English books, math books, history papers. Everything I could think of until he finally realized that my life was important.

Argh!

I pulled my pillow over my face and screamed.

I was a failure.

A total failure.

I couldn't make The Homework Club work. Not by myself. Not with anyone's help. I had to e-mail Mr. Walker and tell him I sucked and couldn't do it.

Might as well do it now. Get it over with.

I kicked off my covers and got up, tripping over a football that Theo had once autographed for me as a joke. What was I doing with that stupid thing? I picked it up, walked over to my window and threw it outside. It landed with a thunk in the bushes.

With any luck, a rabid dog would find it and destroy it before the morning came and I had to see it again.

I booted up my computer and started an e-mail to Mr. Walker.

I got as far as typing his name and then stopped. How could I write that I was a failure? I hadn't failed at anything in my whole life. At least nothing related to school, which was all I'd ever tried.

The cursor sat there blinking at me, waiting for me to put in writing that I was going to let down two student bodies.

But I couldn't do it. I couldn't type those words.

Instead I wrote a hate e-mail to Theo and sent it to myself.

And then I went to bed, none of my problems solved.

Chapter Five

I stayed home sick from school the next day. It was either that or face Allie in homeroom. I couldn't bear to listen to her go on about some cute boy she'd met, or how much fun everyone had had after I left.

No one understood how important this whole thing was to me. Maybe George, but he was more interested in studying than worrying about my newspaper article.

I couldn't face my failure.

I spent the day on the couch. The house was quiet. All my little sisters and brothers were off at school and day care. I had the whole place to myself. No one to bug me or intrude upon my misery.

And when I took one of the pictures of Theo from my nightstand and burned it in the candle that was on the kitchen table, no one was around to tell me to stop.

Sort of made me wonder exactly how evil and bad I

would become if there was never anyone around to tell me to shape up. What would I be like if I didn't have all these responsibilities? Maybe I'd turn into some biker chick who pierced her nipples and had a tattoo on the inside of her thigh.

I almost laughed, picturing myself like that. Maybe throw in a micromini, some fishnet stockings and an overdose of makeup. Can you even imagine what the world would do if I emerged from my bedroom like that one morning?

That would be cool.

Imagine the sense of freedom. I wouldn't care what anyone thought. I wouldn't worry about homework or rotten newspaper articles or anything. I'd just do whatever I wanted to do.

Then I saw my book bag in the corner and reality reared its ugly head.

I was on scholarship. Good grades weren't optional. And I didn't want to fail at this Homework Club!

I sat up. Why did I have to fail? I was smart, wasn't I? Just because I was a freshman girl with no social influence whatsoever didn't mean I should give up, did it? I had other weapons I could use. I simply had to make a choice: make Theo happy so he might like me someday, or forget about the jerk and focus on what was important to me.

After his stupidity at The Homework Club last night, I wasn't feeling particularly altruistic toward Theo.

So forget him.

This was about *me*.

I had weapons, and I wasn't afraid to use them.

I was going to make his parents do the dirty work. I really was. That was my plan the whole way over to the Waller house: tell his mom and dad how he'd screwed everything up and let them deal with making him shape up.

But when I walked into the house, the first thing I saw was Theo stretched out on the couch, watching television. He looked so cool and arrogant—not a care in the world.

Of course he wasn't stressed out. It wasn't his life he was screwing up.

He glanced up and saw me standing in the doorway. He lifted his brows, probably at the sight of the smoke coming out of my ears and the flames bursting from my nose. "Hey, Frances."

Hey, Frances? No apology? Not even an acknowledgement of how he'd messed everything up for me? Nothing?

Suddenly, I didn't care about him anymore. Not as a guy. Not as some cute boy who I'd had a crush on ever since I could remember. He was just a total scumbag! "Theo!"

His gaze flicked from the television back to me. "Yeah?"

"What's your problem?"

He looked a little surprised, no doubt by my hostile

69

tone. Probably because every time I ever spoke to him I'd been worshipping him and wiping drool off my chin. Until now. "What's up, Frances?"

"You!" I marched into the room, grabbed a pillow and flung it at his chest. Nice chest. Too bad it belonged to a jerk.

He caught the pillow and stared at me. "What was that for?"

"You ruined The Homework Club!"

"Oh, *that.*" He tossed the pillow on the floor and relaxed. "I made it better."

"No, you didn't!" I grabbed the pillow again and smacked him in the head. Hard.

"Hey!" He grabbed my wrist and yanked the pillow away. "Cut it out."

"No!" I filched another pillow from the end of the couch, and whacked him right in the face, dodging out of his way when he jumped to his feet. "Don't you realize I'm on scholarship? I have to get good grades. I don't have stupid sports to coast through school on. I have to earn my way, and I needed your help and you let me down!" I hit him again and then leaped sideways, cracking my knee on the coffee table.

Pain rushed up my leg and I hobbled away. Dumb Theo. It was all his fault.

"You okay?"

I glared at Theo. "Shut up! Don't pretend to be nice! You're a jerk and you ruined everything for me."

No way was I falling for some show of thoughtfulness here. He'd failed when it counted.

"Frances, I wasn't trying to screw it up. You wanted people and I got them there. No one would have come if it was to do homework." He sounded annoyed and maybe even a little confused.

Not that I was going to feel bad for him. "Believe it or not, Theo, there are actually some kids who do their homework, who might think that doing it in a coed environment is actually more fun than doing it alone. Homework, that is. Don't give me that dumb look."

"What look?"

"That look that says you've got some crude thought in your head. You can forget it. I'm not interested in you or your stupid ways. Forget about coming to The Homework Club. Keep your horrible friends. I'm going to make this work without you!" I threw the pillow at him as hard as I could, and he caught it easily.

Beast.

"Frances—"

I turned and walked out.

And got as far as the stairs before my legs collapsed.

I was sitting on the bottom step when Allie and Blue came downstairs for dinner a few minutes later. "Frances! What are you doing here?"

What had I done? Screamed at Theo? I never screamed. Ever. Especially not at guys I had a crush on.

Plus I still needed him! I looked at my friends and I had no idea what to say.

"Upstairs." Blue grabbed one arm and Allie latched on to the other and they hauled me up to the second floor and down the hall to Blue's room.

They shut the door, propped me up on the bed and sat down. "What's going on?"

I told them what had happened. Every detail. When I finished, they were both staring at me like I was some freak who had feet growing out of my forehead. "What?"

"I've never seen you like this," Allie said.

"Like what?"

"Yelling."

"And throwing things," Blue said.

I shrugged and flopped back on the bed. They were right. What was happening to me? First, I lied to my parents. And now I'd turned into a psycho? This was not good. Before I knew it, I'd be quitting school to embark on a criminal career. What was I turning into?

"So, what are you going to do?" Allie asked.

Excellent question. "Quit?" But I didn't want to give up. I couldn't give up. Two schools were relying on me! "Kill Theo?" That sounded like more fun. Except that would make me a murderer, and I'd already decided I didn't want to turn to a life of crime. "Go back to my old life?"

Homework on Friday nights? The good little girl?

Somehow that didn't sound so appealing anymore.

"You need to get Theo back on your side," Allie said.

"Yeah, right. That'll be so easy."

"I agree with Allie," Blue said. "You need him."

"Like I need an ice pick in my foot." I decided I hated Theo. He deserved to be hated, so I'd hate him.

"No, seriously, if you want this Homework Club to work, you need his help," Allie said. "You need him to get people there, and you need him to control them."

"Yeah, that'll happen. He's *so* interested in controlling his friends."

Allie clasped her hands behind her back and puffed out her chest. "You have weapons, girl. Use them."

I eyed my friend. "What? Put on some tight clothes and wave my breasts in his face?"

"Exactly." Although a little zing went through me at the thought of doing something like that, I shook my head. "He has girls all over him all the time. He'd be immune."

Allie looked annoyed. "No guy is immune to a girl's body."

My heart jumped. Was there really a chance Theo wouldn't be immune to me as a girl?

"I think Frances is right," Blue interrupted. "Theo wouldn't notice Frances's breasts even if she went downstairs naked."

Great. The one time in my life I would want to be wrong.

"You need to use other weapons," Blue said.

"What weapons?"

"Your brain."

I eyed Blue. "What do you mean?"

"Just think."

I thought.

And then I knew.

But before I could tell my friends about my brilliant idea, a knock sounded at the door. Blue's mom telling us it was time for dinner?

"Frances? Are you in there?"

OMG. It was Theo!

I jumped to my feet, my heart racing, while my friends merely looked annoyed at the interruption. Talk about people who were immune! "I'm in here," I said. Amazing how normal my voice sounded.

This confrontation thing really stressed me out.

"Can I come in?"

Allie glanced at Blue. "You have him really well trained. My sister always barges in on me."

Can't say I'd mind if Theo barged in on me. Except that I hated him. Right. Forgot about that for a minute. "Come in," I said.

I stood up and clenched my fists by my sides. I could do this. I could use my weapons.

The door opened and Theo walked in. Did he look cute, or what? Black jeans, black T-shirt, hair that curled down his neck. He looked rough, and so hot. If I didn't know him so well, I might even be intimidated

74

by him. He gave off the aura of being a bad boy, but inside, he was Theo.

A jerk, remember? "What do you want?" Excellent. I sounded hostile.

He looked at me. "You can't make me stay away."

"From what?"

"The Homework Club. If I want to come, I'll come." His eyes flashed in challenge, and I felt a shiver of excitement rush through me. He'd never looked at me like that, like I was real.

I lifted my chin. "You going to party again?"

"I'll do what I want."

"No, you'll do what I want." OMG. Did I just say that? But this was *my* life at stake and I was going to protect it!

He lifted a brow. "Oh, I will?"

"Yes. You'll come and you'll bring your friends and you'll make them all study exactly the way I tell you to."

He grinned. "Maybe I won't come."

I narrowed my eyes. He only seemed interested in doing the opposite of what I wanted. A control thing? A male thing? Not that it mattered. I was going to win this one. I had one key weapon, and I wasn't going to hold back. "No, Theo. You will come. You will help me. You'll do what I say. You'll do whatever I need."

He lifted his brow. "I don't think so."

"I do." I felt Allie and Blue watching me, but I didn't

dare look at them. I kept my gaze fixed on Theo and tried not to feel terrified.

"Why would I?"

"Because you want to play lacrosse."

He laughed. "What? Are you going to ban me from playing lacrosse?"

"No, but your parents will."

The smile dropped off his face. "What are you saying?"

I'd never realized how good it felt to be evil. I was going to have to incorporate this into my life more often. Total power.

Theo scowled. "What are you talking about?"

"Your parents. You do what I want, or they'll get an earful that might or might not be exaggerated. Whatever it is, it'll be enough to keep you off that team." The beauty of being so close to the Waller family. I knew what his parents were like, and they'd never stand for him letting down his sister, or one of her friends. Which was me.

Theo narrowed his eyes. "You can't do that."

"No?"

He glared at me.

I glowered back.

"You'd really do that?" He did *not* sound happy. Good.

"Yes. But only because you made me. Blame yourself."

For an instant, I could have sworn I saw a flash of

admiration in his expression, but he shoved it away and replaced it with a scowl. "Fine."

Fine? He was surrendering? Impossible. It couldn't be that easy. "Fine, what?"

"I'll come."

"And bring friends?"

He frowned at me. "Yes."

"And not party?"

He looked at me for the longest time, and I could see a tendon flexing in his neck. Finally he said, "We'll have to negotiate."

And then he left.

Wow.

I immediately sank down on the bed, my knees trembling. Allie and Blue stared at me. "What was that?" Allie asked.

"Desperation," I said.

"I guess so." Allie sat down next to me. "I do believe we have a problem, Blue."

"What problem?" Other than the fact I'd become possessed by some psycho girl?

Blue sighed. "I know."

"Know what?" I asked. "What problem?"

"What are we going to do?" Allie asked.

"I don't know," Blue said.

"About what?" I asked.

They ignored me.

"What are you talking about?" My voice held a note of hysteria this time, and still they ignored me.

"We should call Natalie," Blue said.

"Yeah. We may have totally screwed up," Allie said.

Blue's mom shouted up the stairs that it was time for dinner, and my friends got up to walk toward the door.

"Hey!"

They turned around and looked at me.

"What's going on?" I hoped I sounded demanding enough.

Allie and Blue glanced at each other, then back at me. Allie sighed. "The way you just told off Theo?"

"Yeah?" Oh, great. Like I wasn't already stressed enough about that.

"You made him notice you."

I frowned. "So?"

Blue sighed. "No. Not just notice you. *Notice you.*"

I stared. Did they mean that Theo had noticed me? Like as a girl? As someone other than his sister's friend? A shiver of excitement went through me, and then I thought of how he'd ruined The Homework Club. I lifted my chin. "Well, it's too late for him. I already know what a jerk he is. He should have noticed me a month ago." And it was true. He'd pushed me too far.

Allie studied me for a long moment, then she relaxed. "Well, good then. Nothing to worry about."

Why did I feel like she was totally wrong?

A few minutes later, I sat down at dinner across from Theo. He nodded at me, with a nervous flick of his eyes toward his parents.

How about that? He was afraid of me. Or at least, he respected my power.

Interesting.

The question was, what happened now?

I had no idea what to do with power.

Guess I'd better figure it out.

Chapter Six

I got home to an e-mail on my computer from Mr. Walker.

Hello, Frances.
I haven't had any updates from you on The Homework Club, and you missed the last two newspaper meetings. I need to know the status. The article is due in six weeks.

Mr. Walker

Five after seven on Wednesday night.

No one present for The Homework Club except me and my friends.

And George Moon. He and I were in the kitchen, working on an English paper I needed to write, but I couldn't concentrate. I kept listening for the door. Was

Theo going to show up? What was he going to do once he got there?

"So, Frances," George said.

"What?"

He touched my arm, and I looked at him, with his glasses and short red hair. "I was, um, thinking."

I sighed. "About what?"

"Do you want to maybe . . . sort of go to a movie with me on Friday? My mom will drive us."

A date? Like my first real date? I almost fell off my chair.

George's cheeks were bright red and he looked like he'd rather be anywhere but in that kitchen with me.

For an instant, I thought of Theo. And there was nothing. No yearning. No crush. It was over. He'd cured me of my obsession by showing me the side he'd showed everyone else for so long. Which meant I was free. For George.

George was perfect for me. Studious, serious, and a dedicated student. He was my type of boy. So I nodded. "Sure. I'll go."

He grinned and I smiled back.

And then the front door slammed and I heard loud voices. George's face fell. "They're back?"

"Don't worry. They'll study this time." I jumped up from the table and walked to the front hall. All of the same people from last time were there, carrying pizza and soda, CDs and even a Nerf hoop.

Allie jumped in with a couple lacrosse players who were heading off to the living room, while Blue and Natalie sat down on the foot of the stairs.

I folded my arms across my chest and waited.

Theo was the last one in the door, and when he saw me, he stopped.

Dammit. For someone who was totally over Theo, my heart was really pounding right now.

But I lifted my chin and met his gaze. "What's up with all the food and the music?" Which was already blasting through the house.

He narrowed his eyes. "Get off my case. I'm here, aren't I?"

"That wasn't the whole deal."

He walked in, threw his backpack on the ground, grabbed my arm and pulled me into the living room. "Look."

I looked. The Nerf hoop was set up and some people were dancing. The pizza was open on the table and people were eating. "Looks like last time."

"Look closer."

I realized that Theo's hand was still around my arm. Not that I cared.

"Are you looking?"

I forced myself not to think about his hand, and I looked. Interestingly enough, just about everyone had textbooks open. Most of them weren't being read, but they were open. I did hear one couple discussing a paragraph in their physics book.

Progress, but hardly enough to make The Homework Club a success. I turned to Theo. "Is that it?"

He frowned. "What do you mean? They're working."

"You call that working?"

"Yes." He met my gaze.

"I have different rooms assigned for each of the subjects. You can't have things combined like this. It's too confusing!"

"For who?"

"Everyone!"

Theo rolled his eyes. "Listen, Frances, I'm helping you out here, but you need to take a chill."

I needed to *what?*

"You want this thing to succeed?" he asked.

"Of course I do. That's the whole point of blackmailing you!"

"At least you acknowledge it."

"What?"

"The blackmail."

"I'm not stupid enough to think you'd actually help me out because you liked me, if that's what you're talking about."

Something crossed Theo's face, but he didn't respond to my statement. Instead he said, "If you want this homework thing to succeed, then you have to relax."

"No, I have to push harder. You guys have no idea how to study."

"No, you're the one who has no idea about how

83

anyone else in this world actually thinks. You're the only one like you."

"Like me in what way?" This was not sounding like he was about to shower me with compliments.

"A study freak."

"I'm a freak?" I mean, I was well aware I was hardly a social diva and I knew that boys weren't exactly falling all over me, but a freak? "George doesn't think I'm a freak."

"George? George who?"

"George Moon." I lifted my chin. "He asked me out on a date."

"Well, good for him. It doesn't change the fact that if you want this thing to work, you need to change." He glowered at me. "Even I can't get people to show up for the kind of night you want to organize. Lighten up, or you're out of luck."

"I don't need to lighten up!"

"No?" His eyes were flashing a challenge.

"I'm perfectly light."

He actually grinned. "Frances, you're the most uptight person I know."

"I'm not uptight."

"Want me to prove it?"

"You can't." Theo proving I was uptight? That didn't sound like a good experience.

"Friday night."

I blinked. "What about Friday night?"

"Be at my house at seven."

"Why?"

"You want my help on this thing?"

"No, I don't *want* your help." Not like I had a choice. Theo was the only pied piper of teenagers I knew. "Besides, I have a date Friday night at seven." Did I sound cool or what? I had a date.

He narrowed his eyes. "With George."

"Uh huh."

"Where?"

"Movies."

He lifted a brow. "You really do have a date?"

"Well, of course I do. Apparently, being studious is attractive to the right type of guy." I glared at him. "So there."

He shrugged. "Whatever."

He started to turn away and I grabbed his arm. "So, are you going to make them turn off the music and put away the food and work? I have a schedule."

"No."

"No, what?"

"You're pushing it too far. Change or fail. Call me when you decide." And then he walked out the door and slammed it behind him.

And to think Theo had girls falling all over him. I simply couldn't see it happening.

But that was fine he was gone. The Homework Club was all mine now.

I walked over to the stereo and turned it off, prompting a number of protests. I held up my hands, and suddenly realized that I was a freshman in a room full of seniors, and I'd just turned off the stereo.

Had I lost my mind?

This was why I needed Theo's help.

Then I scowled. I didn't need his help. I'd show him I was right. People would discover how much fun it was to study. And everything would be good. I held up my schedule. "Thanks for coming. There are specific rooms designated for each subject." I started to rattle them off, but no one moved. They just stared at me.

I cleared my throat. "We'll study for forty-five minutes, and then there will be a rotation." I sought out Allie, who was in the corner with some guy. "Allie, will you take down the Nerf hoop, please?"

Some tall guy moved in front of it to block it, and Allie glanced at me, and sat down.

Great. Mutiny by one of my best friends.

"So, where's the fun?" a redhead asked.

"This isn't about fun. It's about homework. You guys will get better grades. What more do you need?"

"Not this." The Nerf hoop guy grabbed the hoop off the door, picked up his backpack and a textbook and walked out.

The redhead followed him.

And in about thirty seconds, the house was empty.

"That was impressive," Allie said. She hadn't moved from her spot. "I've never seen anyone end a party so quickly."

"It wasn't a party." Why couldn't anyone understand that?

"You need to chill out, Frances," Allie said.

What? Allie too? "But . . ." I wasn't uptight, really I wasn't. I just had responsibilities and I was trying to do a good job and . . .

I turned to the stairs, where Blue and Natalie were still sitting. "Do you guys think I'm too uptight?"

Blue shifted. "You do study a lot."

"Natalie?"

She looked at Allie and Blue, then sort of shrugged. "You might be a little rigid sometimes."

Unbelievable.

Total betrayal by my friends.

And then George walked into the foyer. "I have to take off too."

George! He liked me the way I was! "Thanks for coming, George."

"Friday night, then?"

"Yes." I'd show everyone. I could have a social life being myself. So there!

"So, I'll e-mail you for directions to your house?"

"Sure."

He sort of glanced at my friends, then ducked out.

I glared at my former friends. "See? I have a date. How many of you have a date Friday night?"

My expression kept Blue from piping up that she no doubt had a date with her perfect boyfriend.

"So, on Friday, maybe George and I will discuss plans for a new Homework Club for people who actually take school seriously." A club that obviously wouldn't include my friends. "Bye."

And I walked out.

Alone.

And I felt horrible.

"You aren't going out with this boy on Friday," my mom said.

This was turning out to be the worst day of my life. "His mom is driving us. What can happen?"

My mom shook her head. "You're fourteen. Too young to date."

"Mom!"

"You can date when you're eighteen," my dad said.

"Eighteen?" *Eighteen?*

"Right now, you need to focus on school. Plenty of time to date when you're older." My dad picked up his fork and resumed eating the meatloaf my mom had kept warm for him after his late shift.

"I don't need to study every minute of every day."

My dad looked up sharply. "Words like that will get you grounded."

"So, that's it then? No dating? Ever?"

"School, Frances. Do you really want to end up like your dad or me, working so many hours we barely get to see each other, let alone our kids? Living in a house that's too small for our family? No. You're going to do better, and it starts now. Everything you do matters. You can't waste time on boys."

"Maybe I don't want to study all the time." My parents were insane! How could they do this to me! I was their perfect child and they were still treating me like I was some irresponsible deviant? Did they have any idea what I went through to live up to their standards?

"That's it. To your room. Now. You can come back when you're prepared to be constructive."

"But . . ."

My dad pointed to the stairs. "Now."

I slammed my chair back and stomped out of the room. Stupid tears. Why was I crying? Just because Theo thought I was an idiot, and my friends had disowned me, and I wasn't allowed to go on a date with the *one* person in the entire world who thought I was cool the way I was.

Eighteen? Were they kidding?

I slammed my feet on each step and threw my door closed as hard as I could, managing to knock a science award off the wall. Stupid science award. If I was dumb, none of this would be my life. I'd be at public school with no scholarship worries, no pressure for college.

I flung myself onto my bed and pulled a pillow over my face.

"I hate my life," I screamed into the pillow.

Was it any wonder I was the way I was? I had no chance. No hope. By the time my parents were finished with me, I was going to be so socially retarded that I wouldn't even be able to hold down a job.

It was Friday night.

Eight o'clock.

I was supposed to be on my date with George.

But no.

I was home. With no friends, since I still wasn't speaking to any of them. Except to tell them I'd been banned from dating until I was too old to walk. Things that horrible had to be shared.

I was supposed to be downstairs helping control my ninety million siblings while my mom made dinner, but fat chance of that. Destroying my life wasn't going to result in slave labor for them.

Too bad I hadn't swiped any food before my self-imposed exile in my room. I was already starving.

A thud sounded on my window, jolting me to my feet in a terrified leap. What was that?

Another thud sounded, and the windowpane shook.

Holy cow. I was being stalked by some evil specter that was floating around my second-floor window. I started backing toward my door.

Another thud, and this time I saw something yellow fly by the window.

A yellow evil specter? Anything evil should be black.

I grabbed a thick math book as a weapon, then edged toward the window. Maybe it was George Moon, here to declare his love for me and whisk me off into some fairy-tale land. Doubtful, but might be worth a look.

I reached the window and peered out. Too dark to see anything with the reflection from my lights.

My heart racing, I tugged the window open, keeping my math book handy.

Nothing flew in through the window and grabbed me by the throat.

So I stuck my head out. "Hello?"

"Hey."

"Theo?" My heart wasn't about to slow down with Theo in my backyard. "What are you doing here?" I could barely see his outline in the dark.

"Friday night. Your opportunity to prove you aren't uptight, remember?"

Why was he here? "I told you I had a date."

"Well, you don't now, do you?"

Good point. Blue was in trouble for telling him. How could she betray my secrets to the enemy? Total traitor.

"So? Are you coming?" Theo asked.

"Coming where?"

"Out."

Out.

With Theo.

There was a day not so long ago when I would've died for that chance.

Not anymore.

Plus, "I'm not allowed to go out with boys." Even ones who were total jerks.

"My point exactly."

"What are you talking about?"

He moved forward into the light from the back porch. He was wearing his black leather jacket with the collar up, and he looked really hot. "Sneak out," he said.

"What?"

He grinned, and I could see his white teeth flashing at me. "Or are you too uptight?"

"I'm not uptight."

"Then come out."

A shiver of excitement suddenly burst through me. Sneak out? I couldn't do that.

"Are you coming?"

I looked down into my backyard. There stood a boy who represented the antithesis of everything about me. He didn't study, he had girls all over him, he didn't respect me or anything I stood for.

And suddenly I wanted nothing more than to pretend I wasn't Frances Spinelli, scholarship student. I wanted to be Frances Spinelli, high school dropout with no parents.

"Frances?"

I stared at Theo. I couldn't do it. Lying to my parents about The Homework Club was one thing. At least that was designed to improve my college application. It was for my parents' benefit, even if they couldn't see that.

Sneaking out with Theo to prove I wasn't uptight?

No.

That wasn't me.

"If you want that club of yours to succeed, you're going to have to listen to me," Theo said.

Figured. Blue probably told him what had happened when he left. I was never speaking to her again.

He shrugged. "Fine."

And then he turned away. I watched him walk to the corner of the house. "Theo!"

He glanced over his shoulder at me.

"I'm coming. I'll meet you out front."

I could see his grin even in the dark and then he disappeared.

Oh my God.

What had I done?

Chapter Seven

I slammed the window shut, my heart racing. I couldn't do it. Take off with Theo when I was forbidden to date? I wasn't even allowed to ride in a car with a freshman boy and his mother, yet I was going to sneak out with a senior who had his own car?

Impossible.

So not my thing.

Said even as I shoved my sneakers onto my feet and grabbed my coat. A quick glance in the mirror told me my hair was a hopeless situation and I shouldn't even bother.

So I didn't.

It was Theo, after all.

The enemy.

It would hardly do to look like I was trying to impress him.

I made it as far as the top of the stairs, and then I

ran back into my room and quickly brushed my hair. Couldn't hurt to be presentable, right? Had nothing to do with Theo as a guy.

I didn't bother with makeup, though. Why start something new? Didn't have any anyway.

I ran to the top of the stairs and paused. The twins were screaming, my mom was trying to soothe them and I could hear someone else crying. She'd never notice.

I took a deep breath and crept halfway down the stairs.

You can still turn back, Frances.

I peered through the railing. Only my little sister Dawn was watching me. She'd benefit from this someday. I'd break my parents in, and by the time she was my age, my parents would be too exhausted to rule the house anymore.

Either that or they'd be handcuffing the kids to their computers by then.

I motioned at her to be quiet, and her eyes widened.

I tiptoed down the rest of the stairs, my heart pounding so loud in my ears I thought for sure my mom would hear it.

But no one came out of the kitchen.

Just Dawn, standing there watching me.

I reached the front door and put my hand on the doorknob.

What was I doing?

My mom would figure out I was gone. She'd kill me. *Kill me.*

And if I stayed upstairs and got my homework done, she'd be mollified and soon forget I wasn't allowed to emerge from the house in the presence of a boy. Next time I'd present it as a study evening, and then she'd let me go. But if I snuck out, then I'd seriously be grounded forever.

It was much smarter to go upstairs.

Don't go out, Frances.

I opened the door and slipped outside, closing the door softly behind me.

Theo stood, leaning against the front gate, his arms folded across his chest. He wore all black. Jeans, leather jacket, boots, gloves and a baseball cap.

Somehow, that baseball cap took all his toughness away. It was just Theo, even with his hair blowing in the cold wind and too much stubble on his jaw for anything proper.

"You made it."

I lifted my chin. "You sound surprised."

"I am."

As I walked toward him, he levered himself off the gate and pushed it open for me. "After you."

I nodded and walked through, quickly glancing over my shoulder at the house. Dawn was standing in the window watching me.

I was going to be so busted when I got home.

"You want to change your mind?" Theo had stopped and was looking at me.

Yes. "No."

"Good." He moved over to his car and opened the passenger door for me. "Hop in."

"Where are we going?"

"A surprise."

Don't get in the car, Frances. He's some senior who's about to take you somewhere to prove you aren't uptight. What good could possibly come of this? I got in.

Nothing was going to stop me tonight.

Theo tucked my feet inside the door, then shut it gently. As he made his way around the car, I looked again at my house. Dawn was no longer in the window. Had she gone to tell my mom?

Theo got in, and the car shifted under his weight. He shot me a grin and started the engine.

What was I doing? Had I gone insane? Theo was a "bad boy" and I was sneaking out on a Friday night with him? How did I know he wasn't going to drive me off into some graveyard somewhere and try to have his way with me or something? Isn't that what guys like him did?

I felt faint. My heart started racing again and my hand moved to the door handle to open it and run for safety.

And then he fastened his seatbelt.

His seatbelt.

Mr. Bad Boy wore a seatbelt.

And that's when I knew I would be safe with him.

So I put mine on too and grinned. "Where to?"

He said nothing. Only flashed me an elusive smile and shifted into drive.

Just as we were pulling away from the curb, I saw the front door of my house open and my mom came out on the porch.

There was no turning back now.

I was a bad girl.

And I didn't care.

Homework was sitting in my book bag, undone. My mom was warming up the gallows for when I got home. And I didn't care.

He hopped onto the turnpike, and I knew we were heading into Boston.

Wow. Boston on a Friday night with a hot guy. And to think I'd seriously considered staying home with my textbooks. Maybe there was something to not always being good.

Maybe. I still felt guilty.

We rode in silence for twenty minutes, during which time I started to feel more and more uncomfortable. I had nothing to say. Why? Because I was boring and uptight and totally out of my element. Who was I kidding? This wasn't me. "Maybe you should just drop me off at your house. I'll go hang with Blue."

He shot me a look I couldn't read. "She's out with Colin."

"Oh." I digested that. "How about Allie's house? Or Natalie?"

"What's wrong with me?"

He was watching the road, so I couldn't see the expression on his face at all. Was he kidding? Mocking me?

"You're a jerk."

He grinned and glanced at me. "When did you decide that?"

"When you screwed up The Homework Club and didn't care."

"And before that?"

I frowned. "What do you mean?"

"Before I did that. Did you still think I was a jerk?"

No, I had the hugest crush on you. As if I was going to say that. "Your reputation precedes you. You're quite well known as a jerk."

"Huh."

What was he thinking? I couldn't tell at all, but he wasn't being the normal Theo.

"You didn't put on any makeup tonight."

"So?" Oh, great. So now he was going to start telling me how young I was because I didn't wear makeup? "That's because I don't care what you think of me." Which was true, and it felt good. Not caring was powerful!

He shot me a look, and I shot him one back. Then he turned into a parking garage, and didn't say anything until he had parked the car and turned off the ignition. Then he turned toward me, and sort of rested his left arm casually across the steering wheel. "You aren't playing games, are you?"

"Games?"

"You honestly don't care."

"About what?"

"Impressing me."

He sounded so surprised I almost laughed. "A first for you, huh?"

"Never really thought about it."

So, this was the way to Theo's heart? Scream at him, ban him from The Homework Club, blackmail him, turn down his invitation for a night out, and generally act like he was a royal pain in the butt?

Now that I thought about it, ever since I'd blown up at him in the living room, he'd been trying to insert himself into my life.

Which probably meant that if I *did* fall victim to his charm, then he'd be back to the old Theo and I'd be another one of his conquests.

Well, forget that. I was so not going to be another girl used and dumped by Theo. Besides, he *was* a jerk. Didn't study, wanted every girl on the planet to worship him and encouraged me to engage in deviant and deceptive behavior.

So I didn't like him. I didn't want to impress him. And I certainly wasn't going to feed his ego.

I was here for one reason only: to prove I had the right approach to The Homework Club.

Hang on. How did being deviant prove I was right about The Homework Club? No, I was certain there was some constructive reason I was out with Theo. Just couldn't recall it right now.

Theo opened my door, and I realized he'd gotten out and walked around his car already. For a jerk, he had pretty good date manners.

Not that this was a date.

Besides, he was probably just trying to feed his ego by wooing me.

Well, he could just forget it.

I was here to prove to him that I wasn't uptight, that my plans for The Homework Club were reasonable and that he was the irresponsible one who was off target. And then when he saw I was actually the balanced one and he was the extreme, then he'd be forced to admit I was right. And *then*, he'd have to agree to help me run The Homework Club the way I wanted to, so success would be mine.

See? I knew I had a good reason for being here.

"Ready?" he asked.

"Sure."

"Good." He grabbed my hand and led the way through the parking garage.

My hand? He grabbed my hand? What was that all about?

I knew what it was about. His ego. Couldn't deal with the fact I wasn't drooling over him anymore. Figured with a little bit of attention, I'd fall at his feet, a dramatic return to the old, adoring Frances.

Well, forget that. I was immune.

But I suppose it couldn't hurt to let him keep holding my hand. I mean, not for his sake, but why not? I sort of liked it. Not him. It. Having my hand held by some hot guy. In public. It didn't matter at all that it was *Theo* who was holding my hand.

Yeah.

We walked down the sidewalk to a place with a line out front. Looked like a bar or something.

A bar? I couldn't go to a bar! I was like seven years too young!

He walked past the place, and I relaxed.

"Afraid of going in there?" he asked.

Jerk. How dare he notice I'd gotten nervous? "Not at all."

"Good. Because that's where we're going."

OMG. "But I'm fourteen."

He stopped and grabbed me by the shoulders. "Don't say that again, okay? If someone overhears you, you'll blow our cover."

"But . . ."

"You wanted to come, so you have to go along with it."

I lowered my voice, trying not to think about how good his hands felt on my shoulders. "But there's no way I can pass for twenty-one."

"This club is for eighteen and over. You can pass for eighteen if you're with me."

He reached up and brushed my hair forward, so it sort of fell over my face. "There. You look sultry and gorgeous. Your dark coloring is really exotic. Just look snobby and bored to be here and no one will question your age."

Sultry?

Exotic?

Gorgeous?

And he'd touched my hair!

Okay, Theo was obviously better than I thought at making girls succumb to his charm. Time to think again how miserable that Homework Club was, and how he totally blew off everything that was important to me.

Yeah.

Yeah!

He grabbed my hand again and pulled me down an alley.

I was too busy practicing my annoyed and sultry look to worry that we were going to be mugged by some psycho jumping out from behind a Dumpster. Besides, Theo was over six feet tall. Who was going to mess with him?

We stopped outside a black door. Theo fixed my

hair again, my knees got a little trembly, and then he smiled at me. "Just go along with what I say."

"Right."

He put his arm over my shoulder and pulled me against him. Hard against him. Like, I could feel his whole body against me, even through our coats. Wow. Talk about zings going through my stomach.

Theo banged on the door. Then he fixed my hair again. "Keep it draped over your face," he said.

Or not. If I kept pushing it back, then he'd have to fix it again.

This was turning into some kind of interesting night.

The door opened to reveal a really big guy who looked vaguely familiar.

He nodded at Theo, then glanced at me. "Who's this?"

"My girlfriend."

The dude sort of smirked, a look that said, "Yeah, you have a lot of those."

Nothing like a reminder that you're out with a player.

Boys. Total nightmares.

Theo handed him what looked like two or three twenties, and then the guy stepped aside. "Come on in."

Unbelievable. We were going to sneak into a club, both of us underage, through bribery. Where was my brain? There was no way I was going in there.

Then Theo tightened his arm around my shoulders, and we walked inside.

Okay, I was inside, but no way was I going to stay.

Theo grabbed my hand and held it out. Big Guy stamped the back of it, and then did Theo's. And then he thumped Theo on the shoulder and walked away.

Leaving us in the back hall of some over-eighteen club.

"What was that about?" I asked. "Bribery?"

"He was captain of the football team my freshman year at Mapleville. We've stayed in touch."

Oh, great. That male athlete bonding thing. Gotta love that.

That did explain why he looked vaguely familiar though. . . .

Theo unzipped his jacket.

"You aren't seriously thinking of staying?" I asked.

Theo lifted a brow at me, then shrugged off his coat. "Yep."

"But . . ."

He grinned and unbuttoned my jacket and tugged it off my shoulders. "Leave your stuff here. We'll come get it before we leave. They'll get stolen for sure if we take them off out there."

Theo had undressed me. Granted, it was just my coat, but come on! No guy had every taken anything off me before. Ever!

Then he grabbed my hand *again* and led the way

down the dark hallway, as if he knew exactly where he was going.

"You've done this before."

He grinned at me. "Yep."

"Always with a different girl?"

"Not always. Occasionally, there's a repeat." He lifted his brow. "Jealous?"

"Not a chance."

Something flashed across his face, and he didn't look quite so amused anymore.

But he also didn't let go of my hand.

And when he pushed open another door and we walked out into the club, I almost passed out from terror right then.

It was dark. Really dark. And loud. Music was blasting so loud I could actually feel it vibrating in my chest and thudding in my ears. And there were people everywhere. Not boys and girls. Men and women. Dancing. Wearing black and silk and some of the women weren't wearing all that much at all. No one even looked close to my age, and there sure wasn't any woman there without makeup, wearing jeans, sneakers and a baggy cotton sweater.

Except me.

Holy cow.

"Want a drink?" Theo asked.

"No." I pulled my hand out of his and backed against the wall. Oh my God. What kind of place was this? Where had I let him take me? It was one thing not to be uptight, but this was something else entirely.

I was way out of my league.

Look at the people on the dance floor! Going crazy! Making out! There was no way I was going out there!

Then Theo moved in front of me and blocked my view. "Frances? Are you okay?"

"No!" I shoved at his chest, and he caught my hands. "Let go of me! How could you bring me here?"

"Sorry."

The simple comment caught my attention, and I stopped railing long enough to look at him. "No smug remark that it proves I'm uptight?"

He shrugged, *still holding my hands.* "I didn't mean to scare you."

He sounded like he really meant it. I didn't understand. Where was this Theo coming from? He was like two different people. "Why aren't you being a jerk?"

A grimace pulled at the corner of his mouth. "I don't know."

"Oh." Not the best answer.

"You want to leave? We can leave."

"Well . . ." Now that he was being all nice, and blocking my view of the raunchy stuff happening on the dance floor, it didn't seem so bad to be there.

"Want to just hang here, against the wall, for a few minutes while you decide?"

I nodded. "Fine."

He gave me a slight nod, then dropped my hands and moved to the wall beside me, leaning against it, his arm pressing against my shoulder. Like he was being supportive.

We stood like that for a while. I watched the people, thought about Theo still leaning against me, not saying anything jerky or anything. Just hanging.

No one came up and bothered us. No one pointed at me like I stood out as being the only fourteen-year-old in the place.

"How are you feeling?" Theo asked.

"Okay."

"Want to dance?"

I looked at the floor. It was a slow song. "No."

"Why not?" He moved to stand in front of me again, but he didn't take my hands or anything. "I won't try anything."

"I just don't want to."

"You ever slow danced with a guy before?"

I lifted my chin. "None of your business."

He shrugged, but there was that challenge thing blazing in his eyes again. "One dance."

"Why?"

"Education."

I almost laughed. "What kind of a line is that? You use that on all your dates?" Not that we were on a date, or anything.

"The Homework Club." He didn't acknowledge the date remark.

"What about it?"

"You can't run it the way you want to."

I lifted my chin. "Yes, I can."

"I brought you here so you can see what else is out there. So you can see why your approach is too hard-line. My friends know how much fun a coed environment can really be. You need to play on that, instead of denying it."

"Since when did you become a philosopher?"

"Since you threatened to get me kicked off the lacrosse team. No way am I going to let that happen. And if the only way I'm going to get to play lacrosse is to get this club of yours to work, then that's what I'm going to do."

"Oh." That's all tonight was about. His desire to keep playing lacrosse. Which was fine. The only reason I was here was for The Homework Club.

So why did I feel so disappointed? I didn't even like him, remember?

"So . . ." He took my left hand. "In order for you to understand what changes need to be made, you have to see how the other side lives."

I eyed him. "Sounds like another line to me."

"I wouldn't waste a line on you."

"What does that mean?" *That I'm not worth it? That you have so little interest in me that you wouldn't want me to succumb to your charms?*

"Because you'd probably kick me in the nuts."

I laughed. "Probably. You are a womanizing jerk."

"See? I knew it." He grabbed my other hand and started walking backward, pulling me with him. "One dance. For research's sake."

One dance.

For The Homework Club.

"Fine."

A nice smile lit up his face, and he dropped one hand and turned to lead me out on the dance floor.

Where his arms would soon be around me.

Chapter Eight

By the time we got to the dance floor and all the older people around me were seriously getting it on, I had totally changed my mind. "Theo."

"Yeah?" He turned toward me, put his arms around my waist, pulled me near him and started swaying to the music.

Huh. Was that it? He wasn't going to try to make out with me? I glanced around, but no one seemed to care about us. No one was looking at my attire and wrinkling their nose.

"What is it, Frances?"

"Nothing." I put my arms around his neck and let him lead me around the floor. This was okay, dancing with Theo. I kind of liked it, actually. In an impersonal way, of course. Not that I was particularly liking the fact it was Theo, just the dancing. Just having a guy's arms around me.

"Relax."

"Sure." I sort of looked around again, and I saw that for the couples who weren't actually making out, the girls all had their faces sort of mashed into the guy's chest. Why not? Theo had a chest too, didn't he? Might as well use it.

So, I moved a tiny bit closer and turned my face to the side and rested my cheek against his T-shirt. I could feel his heart beating, and I was quite aware that he tightened his grip on my waist and pulled me a little nearer.

And you know what? I didn't mind. Kind of liked it, actually.

I burrowed my face deeper against him and realized that being in a guy's arms was pretty sweet. Or maybe it was because it was Theo. Or not. Preferably not.

Then I felt him kiss the top of my head.

Holy cow. I wasn't going to have to stomp on his foot and poke his eyes out, was I?

He kissed my head again, and then I felt his lips on my neck, sort of sliding along and nibbling. My stomach immediately started getting all jittery and my heart was racing. Theo was totally trying to get it on with me!

For an instant, I was totally tempted. Why not? What did I have to lose?

The Homework Club. My future.

And any chance of ever having Theo's interest. When had he started to help me? When I yelled at him. When I showed him I wasn't buying into his aura. When I told him I didn't need him for anything.

If I started making out with him, he'd have what he wanted and walk away.

Well, forget it.

He caught my earlobe between his teeth, and I almost changed my mind. No wonder Allie kissed a lot of boys.

No. I had plans. *Get it together, Frances.*

I pulled back from him, and Theo caught my face in his hands.

He was going to kiss me. Really kiss me. I could see it in his eyes and his mouth and the way he'd gone all soft in his face. Almost tender. Theo, tender? I never would have thought it.

Resist, Frances. "Don't."

He paused, his mouth only an inch from mine. "What?"

I put my hands on his wrists. "Don't."

"Don't kiss you?" He sounded confused.

"Exactly." I tightened my grip on his and tugged. He let me take his hands off my face, and more than a small surge of regret whooshed through me. "I'm not here to become one of your conquests."

"My conquests?"

"Would you stop repeating everything I say?" The music ended and switched to a faster song. "Let's just dance."

"You aren't a conquest."

I rolled my eyes and danced away from him. Funny how a few weeks ago, an almost-kiss from Theo would probably have caused me to pass out. Nothing like having him take away my future for the crush to fade.

And it wasn't just that.

I wasn't a fool. I knew the only reason he was interested was because he couldn't have me. And once he had me, I'd be history, like all the other chicks. I'd known Theo since I was three. I *knew* him. Never bothered to really assess him until now, but I definitely knew him.

I had too much pride to be kissed and thrown away, even if it was Theo. Who needed boys anyway?

Well, I did, but only as study partners.

Theo caught up to me, and grabbed my wrist. I spun toward him, wiggling my hips like Allie had taught us. I put my arms over my head, aware that my sweater was probably creeping up. Showing a little skin, maybe? I might be wearing sneakers, jeans and no makeup, but I was still a girl. Might as well let Theo know what he wasn't going to get.

He grabbed me and pulled me up against him, moving in time to the quicker beat. "You're impossible."

I lifted my brows and set my hands on his chest, ready to block him even as we danced. "What does that mean?"

"I can't figure you out."

Ah. A woman of mystery. I loved it. "You've known me your whole life. What's there to figure out?"

"Have I?" He trailed one finger over my collarbone and sort of down toward my breast.

I grabbed his hand and diverted it. "Of course you know me."

"I think maybe I don't. I thought I did, but . . ."

I broke his grasp and spun away from him. This was *way* more fun than dancing with my friends around Allie's living room. Then I promptly crashed into some other guy, who whirled around and started dancing with me.

Huh.

Okay.

I started dancing with him. He looked about twenty, had blond hair cut short. He was wearing jeans and a button-down shirt, a total prep. Nothing like my bad boy Theo in his black clothes and shaggy haircut. This guy was way more my type. Probably did his homework and everything.

Then Theo grabbed my wrist and turned me back toward him, immediately anchoring his hands around my waist and hauling me against him. "You're here with me."

Why not? I threw my hands around his neck and danced. "You're arrogant."

"I don't share my woman."

"I am *so* not your woman."

"They why are you dancing with me?"

"Education." I couldn't stop the grin that came over my face at his sullen look. "What? Did you think I wanted to get in line for the make-out-with-Theo-and-then-get-dumped parade?"

He frowned. "How do you know I'd dump you?"

I twisted my fingers in the hair at the base of his neck. "When have you ever not dumped a girl?"

His scowl deepened and he said nothing.

"See? That's what happens when you hang with an intelligent girl, Theo. She's too smart to get sucked into your scheme."

He kissed my forehead. "I always knew there was a reason I hated anything to do with studying."

Okay, so now my forehead was on fire. Maybe I did want to get used and dumped by Theo after all. Or not.

Then he kissed my nose, and I started to forget to keep moving with the music. "You're a jerk," I said.

"Not always." Then he kissed my left cheek.

"And you treat girls badly."

"Not always." He kissed my right cheek.

"I'm not one of your women."

And then he kissed me on the lips. A real kiss. Lips, tongue and everything. And I kissed him back. Hard. And I couldn't hear the music anymore. I didn't feel any of the other dancers bumping against us. All I could feel was Theo's hands on my back, moving and caressing. And his lips on mine. And his tongue in my mouth.

And I never wanted to stop. Ever.

His hands were on my shoulder blades, then my lower back, then one was on the back of my neck, and then on my butt. . . . My butt!

I wrenched myself away from him and backed away.

My legs were shaking, I could barely breathe, and my heart was racing. Racing!

And Theo didn't look smug at all. Good thing, or I totally would have kneed him in the groin. He was looking a little confused and dazed, exactly how I felt. I drew in a rattled breath and touched my lips.

Unbelievable.

That had been amazing.

Theo held out his arms and I backed away again.

"Where are you going?"

"You grabbed my butt."

He grinned, back to his cocky self. "I know."

"Jerk. You had to ruin it, didn't you?"

He didn't look contrite. "Grabbing your butt ruined it?"

"No." It just scared the hell out of me. "You ruined it by getting that stupid look on your face, like you just won by getting me to kiss you." And he had. For a minute, I thought he'd felt all the same emotions that I'd felt from that kiss. But now, he looked cocky and arrogant, like I was another one of his conquests. "But that's okay. I wouldn't want to forget what you're really like."

I needed some water. To dump on my head. Or his head. One or the other. Didn't really matter which. Just something to get myself to stop thinking about Theo's kiss and his arms around me.

So I turned and walked away.

Theo caught up to me in about two seconds. "Where are you going?"

"To get some water." I didn't look at him. How could I? I'd probably attack him if I looked at him again.

"I'll get it."

I shot him a glance. "You're still a jerk."

"Apparently."

That was the first time he hadn't at least partially denied the accusation. Not sure what that meant.

He stopped next to an empty table. "Save this table. I'll be back with drinks."

I sighed and agreed. For a scumbag, he was being awfully nice.

But he was still a butt-grabbing, arrogant jerk.

It took Theo almost twenty minutes to get our drinks and return, giving me plenty of time to forget about his kiss and his touch. I even had the opportunity to do some crowd-watching.

Theo set my water on the table and sat down next to me, not trying to touch me or anything.

Which was fine.

"So," he said.

"What?"

"I guess we should talk."

About the kiss?

"About The Homework Club," he said.

"Oh, yeah."

He took a sip of his soda. "That's why we're here. For The Homework Club."

"I know."

"So, did you enjoy the kiss?"

"What?" I promptly sprayed the water I'd been drinking all over the table. Theo just grinned and handed me a napkin.

"The kiss? Did you enjoy it?"

"What kind of a question is that?" I wiped the table and tried to keep from falling off my chair out of shock.

He leaned back in his seat and fixed his gaze on me. "The point of tonight was to make you understand how much fun girls and guys can really have. Assuming you agree that tonight was fun, I'm hoping you understand that you can't ask guys and girls to study together and not have any fun. Would you really be happy just sitting down with a book and me and having that be it?"

Um, no. But I wasn't going to admit that to him. "You don't count."

"Why not?"

"Because you don't."

"So, you didn't enjoy the kiss?"

Why was he pushing the kiss thing? "It was fine."

"Fine? I gave you the best I had."

I looked up, and for an instant, I thought I heard a catch in his voice, like he'd dropped all pretense and was actually serious. Theo, worried about his kisses? Like he had to worry. My knees wouldn't stop trembling for a week. Not that Mr. Arrogant needed to hear that. The more I ignored him, the nicer he was to me. "But I will acknowledge that tonight was fun in general."

"But not the kiss?"

I almost laughed. He *was* insecure. Good to know. "So, tonight makes me realize two things. One, yes, there can be some serious fun when guys and girls get together. And two, if someone was in the mood to . . . ah . . ."

"Kiss?"

"Yes. Anyway, if someone was in the mood to do that, it would take more than me to stop them."

"So, you did enjoy the kiss?"

Yes, Theo was definitely obsessed. "So, I'll adjust my Homework Club as long as you promise to help. A compromise."

"Why won't you admit you liked the kiss?"

"So, is it a deal?"

"No deal."

I eyed him. "Now what?"

"I'll help you on one condition."

"What's that?"

"You go on a real date with me."

I choked on nothing. If total panic and shock can be called nothing. It took almost a minute to stop coughing. "What?"

"A date. Not an education thing. A date."

I narrowed my eyes. "You're just mad because I won't tell you you're a good kisser."

He shrugged. "Maybe."

"I'll be grounded after tonight."

"For about a day, until you bring home a perfect grade on another test."

True. Good grades counted for an awful lot in my house. "Are you going to grab my butt again?"

"No." He didn't hesitate. "That didn't go over so well."

I grinned. At least the boy was learning. "Let's have a study date."

His face contorted into a grimace. "A study date? That's not what I had in mind."

"Tonight was your world. It was fun and I'd do it again." And I would. It rocked. Even the kiss. Especially the kiss. "But I still have to study and stuff. So you come to my world this time."

"A study date?"

"Yes." I stood up. "You can think on it. I need to get home."

Theo shook his head in disbelief about the study date the whole way back to the car.

And when we got to my house, with the front-

121

porch lights blazing like searchlights looking out for me, he put the car into park and rested his arm over the back of my seat. "Study date?"

"Emphasis on study." Was he going to kiss me good night? And if he tried, should I let him? Or not?

The front door of my house slammed open and my mom came out on the doorstep. So much for the kiss. "Theo, will you do me a favor?"

He lifted a brow. "What?"

"Walk me to the door. If my mom knows I was out with you, she won't freak so badly. You're like my brother."

"I'm *not* your brother."

"No kidding."

My response must have mollified him, because he turned off the car and got out, catching up to me before I'd taken two steps from the car. And the whole way up the walk to my mom, he had his fingers barely touching my lower back.

"Mom."

"Frances."

"You remember Blue's brother, Theo?"

My mom eyed Theo. "Yes."

"Good evening, Mrs. Spinelli." Theo shook my mom's hand and met her gaze. The guy had actually agreed to face my mom for me. That might, just might, make up for the butt-grabbing incident.

"He gave me a ride to their house tonight, and then

back." I took a deep breath. "I decided to study with Blue."

Theo didn't flinch. Simply smiled at my mom, like he had nothing to hide. He'd obviously lied to parents before. Me, on the other hand? I felt like I was going to pass out from terror and guilt.

"Studying? With Blue?" My mom looked doubtful, and a touch relieved.

"Yes." I tried to look sullen. "I was mad at you for not letting me date George tonight. . . ."

Theo coughed and shifted beside me.

"So I left. I shouldn't have done it, but I was mad. I think you're being unfair to treat me like I'm a child and can't handle a date. His mom would have been there!"

Theo made a strangled sound.

My mom gave me a steely look. "We will discuss this tomorrow." She looked at Theo. "Thanks for getting her home safely, Theo. I'm sorry she was a burden."

"No burden." He shot a glance at me, and I hoped my mom couldn't see the message in them. "No burden at all."

I wondered if my cheeks looked as red as they felt. "I'll see you later."

He nodded. "Nice to see you again, Mrs. Spinelli."

"You too. Drive safely."

Theo jerked his chin at me, then ran down the steps. I didn't even have a chance to watch him leave, as my mom leveled me with a glare. "You. Inside. Now."

"Right." I didn't care if I was grounded until I was fifty. It had been so worth it.

For the future of The Homework Club.

And yes, Theo, the kiss rocked.

Chapter Nine

I was sitting at the Waller dining room table across from Theo, and I couldn't stop looking at his lips. His parents were in the kitchen making dinner, and Blue was in the living room watching television with Allie.

Theo and I were discussing The Homework Club, but I couldn't stop thinking about Friday night.

Only forty-eight hours ago, I'd been in Theo's arms. And now I was sitting across from him in the dining room, pretending as though nothing had happened.

I hadn't told my friends. How could I explain what I didn't even understand? Did I like him or not? One minute I did, and then I didn't.

Plus they'd freak. They weren't exactly fans of the Theo/Frances coupling.

"So, music is okay?" Theo said.

I nodded. "As long as it's low. And only in one room, so people who don't want music can leave." I wouldn't be able to study with music, but Theo had insisted some people could.

"You're not doing that stupid room assignment thing again, are you?"

I scowled at him. "Don't call me stupid." See? Theo the jerk again.

"Trust me, I'd never call *you* stupid. I just think the room assignment thing is." He eyed me. "So? No room assignments?"

"Why do all the girls like you?"

He grinned. "Does it bother you?"

"No." Not much, at least. "I just don't understand it. Calling a girl's ideas stupid is hardly the way to her heart."

"I'm not hoping for their hearts."

Ugh. Nothing like an arrow to the gut on that one. "So, it's all about hooking up, then, is it?" See? I was so glad I hadn't let him grab my butt.

"It's about fun."

"Yeah, whatever." I scowled at my notes. "Food in the kitchen only?"

"Nope. Food anywhere. People like to eat."

I supposed food couldn't hurt.

"And games," he said.

"What, like spin the bottle?"

He lifted his brow. "My friends don't need spin the bottle as a reason to kiss a girl."

Yeah, I guess I knew that. So I had kissing on the brain. Who could blame me?

"I was thinking of study games. Like Jeopardy or something. People pick questions out of the book and quiz the other team. Winner gets a prize," he read from his notes.

Sounded pretty interesting, actually. "What kind of prize?"

He shrugged. "I don't know."

"How about the satisfaction of knowing they know their stuff?"

He gave me a look and I wanted to kick him under the table. "Fine. We'll think of a prize," I said.

Just then, Blue's mom walked into the dining room with the phone. "Frances. Phone."

"Again?" Theo asked.

I rolled my eyes and picked up the phone. "Yeah?"

"Just checking," my mom said.

"I'm still here."

"Good. Blue's mom said you were studying with Theo."

The Homework Club! What if Blue's mom had mentioned we were working on The Homework Club? I was so sunk.

Ah, the life of a liar. It was horrible! "Yeah, he's helping me with my math."

"Good. I'll call back later."

I hung up the phone and stared glumly at it. After the episode on Friday night, my mom had banned me from going anywhere except school and my friends' houses. I could tell she wasn't really sure I'd been at

Blue's house Friday night, but fortunately Blue's parents had been out so they hadn't been able to confirm or deny my story. The solution? I had to tell her where I was going, and she would call at random intervals to make sure I was actually there and working.

Which wasn't so bad, given what the repercussions for Friday night could have been. Especially since The Homework Club was at Allie's, so I could still go there.

But it was just bad and weird to be living a lie to my parents. This wasn't me! It was their fault though. They'd driven me to this by being unreasonable, right? I mean, I was responsible and I deserved a little slack.

"Everything cool at your place?" Theo asked.

"Yeah." I sort of glanced at him. "Thanks for bailing me out Friday night. It helped that you talked to my mom."

He shrugged. "So, when's our real date?"

OMG. He hadn't forgotten. I felt my cheeks heat up and I stared at my notebook. "I'm semi-grounded."

"So? Didn't stop you last time."

I looked up. "Hey! I'm not a total deviant! There are limits. You want a date with me? Well, it'll be on my terms."

He grinned, getting that amused look in his eyes that made him look all soft. Like he liked me. I mean, *liked* me. Too bad he only seemed to get that look when I yelled at him about something. "Anything you want," he said.

"A study date."

He blinked. "You're still on that kick? Are you kidding?"

"Nope. Study date. That's what I do for fun."

"How about a movie?"

"Fine. George Moon wanted to study with me. I'll study with him." A test of my theories. Did Theo like *me* or was it all about winning over a girl who didn't appear interested?

"I'll study with you."

So it wasn't me. It was the fact that he couldn't get me.

That sucked.

What? Was I supposed to play hard to get for the rest of my life? Assuming I cared, of course. He was still a beast.

Well, not all the time. Sometimes he was nice.

And I really liked kissing him.

"So, when?"

"Homework Club is tomorrow night," I said.

"Yeah."

"Why don't we do it Tuesday? That way if you blow it at The Homework Club and I hate you, I can make up an excuse and cancel on you." Actually, it wasn't like I was playing hard to get. I *was* hard to get. I didn't want him. I didn't want to like him. And I was going to say it the way I saw it.

He lifted a brow. "Where?"

"Where to study?"

"Uh huh." He had this sort of suggestive look on his face.

"My house."

He blinked. "Your house? But there's no privacy."

"It's a study date, Theo. Not a chance to hook up." Just saying those words made my stomach quiver. What had he done to me? Turned me into a lust-crazed, lying, deceptive criminal?

It was sort of fun.

"Frances."

I turned around to find Blue and Allie standing in the door, looking stern. "What?"

"How could you have gone out with George on Friday, and not told us?"

I didn't dare look at Theo. "What?"

"My mom said your mom called and said you'd left the house with some guy and that you said it was Theo and he'd driven you over here. I covered for you, but we're all totally offended you didn't tell us. How could you do that?"

"Did you kiss him?" Allie asked.

"Who?" Theo? She knew?

"George, of course. Did you kiss him?"

Theo coughed and I felt panic surging over me. "I didn't kiss George."

I had to tell them. I couldn't handle the lies anymore. It was killing me, and turning me into a worse person by the day.

But then I thought of their reaction. They'd probably lock me upstairs and tell Theo all sorts of horrible things about me to keep me from spending time with him. Well, forget it. I was going to do whatever I wanted, and they weren't going to stop me. So I smiled. "Yes, I had a date with George. It was fun."

"We want details."

Just then, before I could come up with an excuse to hide rather than expand my list of lies to my friends by making up an entire date, Blue's dad came into the dining room and ordered us to start setting the table.

Saved by parents.

I was *so* bailing right after dinner.

Five after seven. Yet again, no one was on time for The Homework Club.

But I sat on the couch in the family room and didn't worry.

Theo would be there with his friends. I knew he would be. It was after he arrived that worried me. What would happen? What if he reverted to the old Theo in front of his friends?

Then he was over. He was done.

The doorbell rang, and I didn't move. Let someone else answer the door. I wasn't going to act like I'd been waiting for him.

Allie shot me a curious look, then got off the couch and answered the door.

It was George.

"George," Allie said loudly. "So good of you to come."

I sat up. I'd forgotten about George. He smiled at me, then sat down next to me on the couch.

"So, what movie did you guys see on Friday?" Allie asked.

"We didn't go out," George said before I could fake a choking attack. "Her parents wouldn't let her."

I felt Allie's eyes on me, but I didn't look at her. At least Blue and Natalie weren't there tonight. Blue had some event with Colin, and Natalie was sick. Allie was the only one I'd have to deal with for now.

"So, um, you ready to study?" I said, tapping George on the shoulder. No need for him to expose any more of my lies.

"Sure." George turned to me. "Since you can't go out, why don't I come to your house and study? Like tomorrow night or something?"

I felt a presence in the room, and I looked up. Theo was standing in the doorway, and he was glaring at George. I mean *glaring*.

"So," George continued, "I could get dropped off at about seven or something. Would that work? We could study until nine?"

I couldn't take my gaze off Theo's face, and he turned to stare at me.

"Frances?" George touched my arm. "So? Is it a date?"

"Yes," Allie said. "Is it a date?"

Theo just stood there. Watching me.

That would be the ultimate slam, to accept George's invite in front of Theo. It'd probably ensure Theo's attentions for at least a week. Especially since Theo and I already had a study date for tomorrow night.

"Frances?"

I looked at George, with his honest face, and knew he'd never ask me to sneak out of my house or get me in trouble with my parents. He'd never grab my butt or anything. He was the right kind of boy for me.

If I had any kind of a brain in my head, I'd accept that invitation right then and let Theo know where I stood. "George . . ."

"Yeah?"

I stole another glance at Theo, and I saw a tendon flex in his neck as he stood there. "Sorry, George. I can't. Not tomorrow."

Theo said nothing. Just turned and walked out of the room.

What? Wasn't he supposed to give some special smile because I'd picked him over George? Or a nod or a wink or something?

Typical Theo.

Jerk.

Fine. I didn't want him anyway. "Let's study, George."

A few kids walked into the room and sat down and pulled out history books. They spread out a three-foot-long sub and ate, quizzing each other between bites.

There was faint music coming out of the living room, and I heard a bunch of laughter coming from the kitchen. "Can you excuse me a sec, George?"

He nodded, looking a little depressed. *Nice, Frances.* Way to hurt his feelings.

I smiled. "Maybe we'll get together later in the week."

He grinned and nodded, looking much more cheerful. "Okay."

"Okay." I left him on the couch and wandered into the kitchen. A lot of kids were in there playing that game Theo had explained to me, and each time someone got an answer wrong, they had to do something stupid that the other team told them to do. Cracking an egg over your own head was the one I got to see.

I almost said something when I saw the food come out of the fridge, but I stopped myself. They were studying, right?

Impressed with my restraint, I walked through the kitchen to the living room. Music was on, Nerf hoop was up, a couple kids were dancing. But the kids shooting hoops were quizzing each other, and only when they got an answer right could they shoot a basket.

And there was a huge debate going on by the coffee table about something that sounded rather juicy, but it was current events, so that was good too.

Then I looked at the dance floor. A couple kids were

dancing, and didn't look much like they were studying. Unless it was sex ed.

Theo was leaning against the wall on the other side of the dance floor, his arms crossed over his chest, looking like he was in a rather foul mood. I could tell the moment he saw me. His eyebrows sort of lifted, and he jerked his chin at the room, no doubt pointing out that people were being fairly studious.

I nodded.

Then he levered himself off the wall and started walking toward me.

My stupid heart started going faster, and my stomach jiggled.

Until some girl got off the couch and wrapped her arms around his waist, cooing about dancing with him. Theo grinned at her, and just when I was ready to walk over there and knock her out with a dictionary, he peeled her arms off and set her back on the couch.

And then kept walking toward me.

Okay, so now I was glad I'd turned down George.

He came to a stop in front of me, so close I could almost feel the heat from his body. "So."

I looked up at him. "Seems to be going well."

"Not too fun?"

"More fun than I would need to have, but it seems to be working."

He grinned.

And I smiled back.

"Come here." He took my wrist and led me back toward the kitchen, stopping in the small hallway between the rooms. From where we were, no one in either room could see us. It was as if we were alone.

He put his hands on my shoulders and pushed me so my back was against the wall, in the corner. He was going to kiss me? Again? With all these people around?

No. I wouldn't let him. I didn't want to kiss him. He was a jerk.

Jerk.

Jerk.

Jerk.

I put my hands on his waist.

And kissed him.

Whoops. Hadn't meant to do that.

But as long as I'd already started . . .

Theo responded instantly, kissing me right back, his hands around my lower back. I was right there with him, matching him with everything I had.

"What are you guys doing?"

I pushed Theo away and spun around. "Allie?"

"Theo!" Allie shoved Theo away from me. "Are you insane?"

Theo didn't look too sheepish. "Hey, Allie."

"You can't kiss Frances!"

"She kissed me."

I shot a mutinous glare at Theo, who looked completely entertained. Well, of course he would. He was a guy, wasn't he? Getting caught hooking up with a girl would do wonders for his reputation. "I didn't kiss you."

"You kissed him?" Allie sounded faint. "But it's *Theo*."

"What's wrong with me?" Theo sounded a touch offended.

"You're a jerk," Allie explained. "Frances needs a nice guy."

Theo scowled. Good. Let him feel bad. "Why does everyone keep calling me a jerk?"

"Because you can be one," Allie said. "Frances, what were you thinking? What about George?"

Theo folded his arms across his chest and looked at me. "Yeah. What about George?"

"He's much more my type," I said.

Theo snorted, and Allie nodded. "Yes, he is," she said. Then her eyes widened. "Was it Theo you went out with on Friday night?"

"Maybe."

Allie spun around, her hands on her hips. "Theo! What are you doing to her? Corrupting her?"

"She's quite corruptible," Theo said, flinching only slightly when I kicked him in the shin. "You really think I could make her do anything she didn't want to do? I fear for my life when I'm with her."

Was that the sweetest thing ever? A guy as tough as Theo respected me. I shot him a smile, and he smiled back.

"You're coming with me." Allie grabbed my arm and pointed at Theo. "You stay away from her."

Theo grinned at me until we were out of sight.

Allie dragged me straight through the living room and up the stairs to her room, where she slammed the door behind us. "What are you doing?"

I just grinned, still thinking about how cute he'd been when he said he was afraid of me. Talk about female power!

"He'll break your heart, Frances. Haven't you been listening to us? Have you had your head under a snowbank for the last ten years, not noticing the string of girls Theo has left behind him? You're too nice for him."

I grinned at Allie. "He's a great kisser."

"Of course he is! He's kissed about a thousand girls!"

Well, when put that way, it didn't sound so good.

Allie sat down next to me on the bed and sighed. "Frances, he doesn't study. He doesn't treat girls well. He's not right for you."

I eyed her. "Maybe you're right."

"Of course I'm right."

"He's coming to my house for a study date tomorrow night."

"So?"

"So, my whole family will be in and out of the room. No way is he going to have a chance to kiss me. It'll really be about studying."

"So?"

"So, maybe there's another side to him you've never seen."

She cocked an eyebrow. "You really like him, don't you?"

"Sometimes."

"And the other times?"

"I think he's a jerk. But when I tell him that, he shapes up pretty well."

Allie studied me. "He did say he was afraid of you."

"Of course he is. I think I'm the only girl he's ever met who doesn't want to climb in the backseat of a car with him." Or at least, not yet. The idea did hold some allure, now that I thought about it. I grinned. "He's turning me into a deviant."

"And that's good?"

I thought for a moment, and then nodded. "He makes me laugh. And have fun."

Allie pursed her lips. "You do have a tendency to be a little too serious."

"So you've said."

"Huh."

We sat there in silence for a few minutes, and then Allie nodded. "Okay, then. As long as you promise to keep him afraid of you and don't climb into any back-seats, this might be okay."

I grinned. "I don't even know if it's going to go anywhere."

"And you're okay with that?"

"Sure. Why not? It's not like I even like him half the time." That was part of the fun. "I'm afraid I don't want to go out with George anymore, though."

Allie grinned. "I wouldn't want to either."

"So, um, do you think we should tell Blue and Natalie?"

Her smile faded. "Blue will freak."

"Like you did."

"Maybe we should wait until we see whether there is something worth freaking her out about."

Phew. "Sounds good."

"But I don't like lying to them."

Join the club. "Me neither." That was the problem with my life right now. It was filled with deception. Lying to my parents about The Homework Club, about Theo, sneaking out at night, not telling my friends stuff, getting into a club through the back door. It was all fun and exciting, and it made me feel terrible at the same time.

Something was going to have to give. I couldn't keep this up.

Chapter Ten

My mom eyed me. "Theo is coming over to study?"

"Yes." How could she possibly object to me doing homework at my house?

"Isn't he a senior?"

"Yes."

"At another school."

"So?"

"So, what homework could you possibly have in common?"

Uh . . .

"And don't even tell me that he's tutoring you. You get straight As."

My mind was totally blank.

"Funny coincidence that it was Theo who picked you up on Friday. And dropped you off."

I felt like I was choking.

"And that Blue's parents weren't home to confirm you were at Blue's house."

Why couldn't my sisters have a crisis right now? Where were the tears? Help!

"And when I called Blue's house on Sunday, you were studying with Theo, according to Blue's mom. Not with the girls. With Theo."

I probably should have had a good lie prepared, but I totally hadn't been expecting to be busted like this.

"So?" My mom folded her arms across her chest and eyed me.

"I'm tutoring him."

My mom narrowed her eyes. "Really." Could there be more skepticism dripping from that word?

"Yes. He's an athlete, and he needs to get his grades up to stay on the team, but he's totally embarrassed. It doesn't do any good for his reputation, you know?" I couldn't believe it. Lying again? What was I turning into? "It's English where he's really struggling. Blue asked me to help him. That way no one at his school has to know."

She just kept looking at me.

I met her gaze, but inside I was crumbling. My stomach hurt and everything felt like it was tumbling down around me. "It'll be great to put on my college application, that I'm a tutor."

"Are you lying to me?"

"No." I couldn't do this anymore. I had to tell her the truth.

She stared at me. "Fine."

Fine?

"He can come over."

I grinned.

"But I'll be watching."

I stopped smiling.

"So, your mom thinks I'm such a bad student that I need a freshman to tutor me?" Theo didn't look too happy after I'd told him the story.

We were sitting in my kitchen, both doors open to the rest of the house.

"What other choice did I have? She knew there was something going on between us."

"But you had to tell her I was stupid?"

"Why do you care? You don't even study."

Theo narrowed his eyes at me. "How do you know?"

"That you don't study?"

"Yes."

"Do you?"

"No."

I grinned. "Then why are you getting upset?"

"My grades are fine. I don't need a tutor."

"Then think what they could be if you studied."

Theo drummed his fingers on the table. "You really take this studying thing seriously, don't you?"

I set my book down. "Yes."

He gestured at the table. "You really invited me over here to work."

"Yes."

He rubbed his chin and looked at me. "So, where's the girl who went dancing on Friday?"

"Same girl." I felt a little lump in the bottom of my stomach. Was this where it ended? He found out what I was really like and decided I was too boring?

"Huh."

"Is that bad?"

He glanced at me, then leaned forward and put his hand over mine. "No. It's not bad. Just different."

Did I believe him?

Then he leaned forward and kissed me quickly.

Okay, I believed him. This just might work.

Three weeks later, we were sitting at my kitchen table again. It was the sixth time we'd studied at my house, and my mom was actually believing me. Theo had started bringing stuff to study and seemed to be taking the work seriously.

Tonight was Friday night, and he was here with me.

A sign, don't you think?

Plus, The Homework Club was going really well. Kids' grades had gone up, and Theo didn't even need to patrol to keep things under control. It was working.

Everything was great.

My mom appeared in the doorway to the kitchen. "We're all going out for ice cream. You two want to come?"

All of them were going? So we'd get the house to ourselves? "No, thanks. We'll keep working."

Theo and I hadn't even been alone together. We only saw each other at The Homework Club, at Blue's house and at my house, since I was semi-grounded and couldn't go anywhere else.

"All right, then. We'll be back in about an hour."

"Bye."

Theo was staring at me.

Neither of us moved until the front door shut. We heard the car start, listened to it pull out, and then sat there for another minute.

Then Theo got a wicked grin on his face, and my heart started racing. "Did I tell you how cute you look tonight?"

I shot him an arrogant look. "No."

"Super cute." He pushed his chair back from the table, stood up and walked over to me. He held out his hand. "Want to dance?"

Like I had to think about that answer for a minute. "No music."

"I'll sing."

Wow. I let him pull me to my feet, and slipped my hands around his neck. He anchored his hands behind my back and pulled me up against him, swaying gently as he started singing softly. It was the same song we'd slow-danced to at the club. "You remember the song we danced to?"

145

"Of course." He kissed my nose, continuing to hum. "How could I forget?"

How indeed? And to think I'd ever called this guy a jerk.

"Mind if I kiss you?"

I grinned. "Maybe."

"Maybe, huh?" He spread his hands on my back, rubbing in a circular motion. I noticed that he kept his hands away from my butt.

Smart guy.

He bent his head, and I met him halfway.

I was becoming quite addicted to kissing.

"Frances!" My mom's squawk ripped into my bliss.

Oh, no. I stumbled backwards, tripping over the chair. Only Theo's quick grab kept me on my feet. Unfortunately, it also ended up with me in his arms.

In front of my mom, who was looking absolutely horrified.

"Mrs. Spinelli, I can explain," Theo said, moving in front of me.

Protecting me from my mom? What a guy. Too bad he was going to find himself in our trash can in about two minutes when my dad walked in.

"You. Out of my house." My mom pointed at Theo. "Now."

"It's not Frances's fault."

"Out!"

Theo glanced at me, and I nodded. "It's okay."

"I'll stay if you want." He was totally ignoring my

mom's howls because he thought I needed him.

I could love this guy. "I'll be fine." Or I'd be dead. Either way, Theo wasn't going to be able to save me.

"I'll call you."

"No, you won't." My mom grabbed his arms and shoved him out the front door, slamming it behind him. Then she turned to face me. "You. Sit. I'm going to go get your father out of the car."

I sat.

My mom left, muttering something about how she'd never been so glad to forget her wallet.

Yeah, me too.

Not.

Allie sat next to me in the cafeteria, listening to my tale of woe. She was the only one I could tell. I wasn't allowed to go to any of my friends' houses, or take phone calls. But my parents couldn't keep me from going to school.

"So, have you talked to Theo since?"

I shook my head. "How could I? My parents won't let me talk on the phone."

"What about e-mail?"

"They took away my modem."

"Wow."

"Yeah."

"What about the computers at school?"

Oh, wow. "Hadn't thought of that." I was *so* going to e-mail Theo after lunch.

"And The Homework Club?"

"Over."

"Bummer."

"Yeah."

My life sucked.

"So, um, I told Blue and Natalie everything," Allie said.

"Do they hate me?"

"No."

I looked at her. "Really? They're not mad I lied to them?"

"They're mad they can't get the details on Theo's kissing."

I grinned. "Really?"

"Swear. I think you might have to grovel a bit, but they'll forgive you."

Phew.

Or not.

What did it matter? I was never going to be allowed to see them again.

The next day when I got to school, I had an e-mail from Theo in response to mine.

Frances! Glad you e-mailed me. Miss you. Take the trash out Friday at nine. I'll meet you in your backyard.—T

Yay!

I was so excited that I e-mailed Natalie and Blue to tell them. I hoped Allie was right that they'd forgiven me, because I needed them in my life again! Some things were so exciting they had to be shared.

And then, because I felt guilty, I e-mailed George to let him know that I wouldn't be able to have any more dates with him.

One minute after nine.

Friday night.

Was Theo in my backyard?

"So, I'll take the trash out." I held up the bag I'd just pulled out of the plastic can under the sink. "Be back in a sec."

My mom waved absently, in the middle of some deep discussion with my dad. Good. She wouldn't notice if I was out there for a few minutes.

I was going to get to see Theo! I was so excited.

I pushed open the back door, then pulled it shut firmly. "Theo?" I whispered, but there was no sound.

Was I early? That would be horrible, because I couldn't hang out in the backyard for an hour waiting for him.

"Theo!"

Nothing.

Jerk. Good thing I wasn't looking forward to seeing him or anything.

I walked down the steps and over to the shed we used for garbage to protect it from the raccoons. I'd just tossed the trash inside and shut the door when I felt a hand snake around my waist and pull me off behind the shed.

I grinned, not exactly fearing for my life.

Sure enough, when I was safely hidden, I turned around to find Theo standing there. "Hi."

He kissed me.

Have I mentioned that I was really discovering the fun of kissing?

"So, you ready?" he asked.

"For what?" Why was he talking? Why couldn't he keep kissing me until I had to go back inside?

"Dancing." He spun me around in his arms, then pulled me up against him.

"Mmm. I wish." I snuggled my face against his chest and realized I wouldn't have too many qualms about sneaking into that club again. Had I become a total deviant or what?

"Seriously. Let's go." He pulled back from me and took my hand to lead me across the yard.

"What?" I yanked my hand free. "You want me to sneak out again?"

"Of course." He stopped and looked confused. "How else are we going to see each other?"

"Theo. I'm already grounded. I can't sneak out."

"Why not? What more can they do to you?"

"They could never trust me again."

"So?"

"So?" I walked over to him and poked him in the chest. "I'll totally admit I've had fun with you, but I can't throw my life away over it anymore."

"Spending time with me is throwing your life away?" He narrowed his eyes and crossed his arms. "Nice."

"No, it's not *you* that's the problem." Yeesh. Boys could be so sensitive. "It's the fact that I have to get my parents to trust me again. I don't want to be grounded for the rest of my life."

"Just keep blowing them off and they'll figure out eventually they have no control over you."

"Said by the boy who never misses a Waller family dinner."

He lifted a brow. "I don't need to rebel. My parents let me do what I want."

"Well, good for you. I have parents I have to deal with, which means not pushing them to the point at which they handcuff me to the computer."

"So, we aren't going to see each other?"

"Theo! What do you want me to do?"

"Fight for me."

"By lying to my parents yet again?" I shook my head. "No way. I'm not doing that anymore." Even though I'd been grounded, it had been somewhat of a relief to be done with the charade. Lying just didn't suit me.

Only, there was still one big lie out there. The Homework Club. Not that I'd ever tell my parents about that one. They thought me dating Theo was the only deception, and they'd get over that as soon as I brought home a few good grades. But if I blew them off again, I'd be in serious trouble for the long haul. "Give me a couple weeks, and I'll get it sorted out."

"A couple weeks?"

"Yes."

Theo shook his head. "Come out with me tonight."

I stomped my foot. "Stop asking me to do that! I can't!"

"Oh, come on, Frances. I thought you were starting to lighten up."

"And I thought you were starting to respect studying."

He glared at me.

I scowled back.

"So you aren't coming tonight?" he asked.

"No." Why couldn't he acknowledge what I had to do?

"Fine."

"Fine." Jerk.

He turned and left.

So I swung around and marched back into the house. As soon as I got released from my grounding, I was going to call George Moon and have a date with someone who actually understood what I was about.

In the meantime, I had an article on The Homework Club to write.

* * *

Two weeks later, I was still grounded, despite bringing home three As. According to my parents, the big issue was the lying. They said they might have eventually adjusted to me dating Theo (gee, thanks for telling me *now*) seeing as how he was Blue's brother and they'd known him for so long. But the fact that I'd totally deceived them about the nature of my relationship with him, including when I'd gone out with him that Friday night? Total betrayal of trust.

They said it could take years to rebuild trust.

Great.

I was sitting at the computer in the library, reading e-mails from Blue and Natalie, who had totally forgiven me and were planning ways to kidnap my parents so I could see all my friends again. And there was even an e-mail from George, who had seemed immensely relieved that the pressure to date was off, and was much happier just being study pals.

All was good.

Except I hadn't heard from Theo since the night at my house, and I was debating with Allie on whether to e-mail him—the same debate we'd been having for the last two weeks.

Allie was sitting next to me. "You know, we did warn you that Theo was too different from you."

"But he's not that different." Sure, he had a wild side, but he did study, got The Homework Club to work, and made me laugh. I liked that he got me to loosen up. Of course, I didn't want to be any more fun than I currently was, and that was the problem. I wasn't quite enough for him.

Sigh.

"Blue told me he hasn't gone out on any dates for the last two weeks."

I glanced at Allie. "Really?" I opened Blue's latest e-mail, and sure enough, same message. "Wow."

"Uh huh."

"That's unusual for Theo."

"That's what we think too."

We. That would be all my friends except me. "I miss you guys."

"We miss you." Allie was sitting backwards in her chair and leaning on it. "Have you tried talking to your parents again?"

"Sort of. Every time I try to bring it up, I get shut down."

A girl walked by us. "Nice job, Frances."

I looked up. "What?"

But she was already gone.

I eyed Allie. "What was that about?"

She shrugged. "I think you should e-mail Theo."

"No. Why should I? He's the one being the jerk."

Another girl walked by and patted me on the shoulder. "Way to go, Frances."

I stared after her. "What's going on?"

Allie twisted around to look at the girl, too. "Did you do something amazing? Burn down the science wing or something?"

"No."

Nicole, a friend of ours from homeroom, ran up to us, waving something. "Oh my gosh, Frances. You're a star!"

I grabbed her wrist so she couldn't take off. "What are you talking about?"

"This!" She thrust a paper into my hand. "Everyone is talking about The Homework Club. There's a delegation from the school newspaper meeting with the heads of both schools at the end of the week to talk about an exchange program. You're a hero!" She grinned at me, then glanced at her watch. "I gotta go. Good job!"

She sped away, leaving Allie and I staring at each other.

After a moment, she took the newspaper out of my hand and opened it.

There was my article, spread across the entire front page. And my name was right there under the title. Frances Spinelli.

Oh, wow.

Allie sat there and read the entire article aloud.

Including the editorial at the end about the proposal for the exchange program and how my article was the first step.

She set it down and grinned at me.

Then we both screamed at the same time, grabbed each other and started dancing around the library. Even getting shushed by the librarian didn't shut us up.

I'd done it!

How cool was that!

The euphoria lasted all day. Kids were telling me "good job" everywhere I went, and even some of the teachers pulled me aside to quietly mention the quality of my article.

I was in!

This was it! My parents would never be able to not trust me again! They'd see how responsible I was and fall at my feet, begging for forgiveness for not trusting me.

And maybe I'd forgive them.

Or not.

And if Theo came crawling back, wanting to hang with me because I was famous? Forget it.

Chapter Eleven

I burst through the front door right after school, the paper in my hand. "Mom!"

It was too early for Dad to be home, but Mom should be there.

"In the kitchen, Frances."

I ran through the house and exploded into the kitchen. My mom and dad were sitting at the table. "Dad! You're home!" Sweet!

"Sit down, Frances."

I suddenly noticed their somber faces. Omigod. Had something happened? "What's wrong?"

"Sit."

I sank down into a chair. "What's wrong?"

"This." My dad pointed to the table. There sat a copy of the newspaper with my article.

What? They were upset about my article? I looked up. "My article?"

"Care to explain?" My dad folded his arms across his chest and my mom gave me this look like I'd totally let her down.

Wow. Nothing like taking away my excitement. Did parents suck or what?

"Frances. Explain."

Fine. "Because of this article I wrote, there's a delegation meeting with the administration of each school to create an exchange program between Field School and North Valley. I've been hailed as a hero all day. Your daughter is a star."

I thought I caught a hint of pride in my dad's face, but my mom was heartless. "That's not what we're talking about!"

I sighed. "What's the problem, then?"

"We banned you from this Homework Club, yet according to this article, you went ahead and did it? Lied to us repeatedly, every time you went?"

Oh. They're upset about *that.* Guess I forgot about that little detail. "You're right."

"So you admit it?" My mom sounded so triumphant I wanted to scream. Why couldn't she be proud of me?

"Of course I admit it. I did The Homework Club anyway. It's your fault I had to lie."

"Our fault?" My mom's voice was heavy with foreboding.

I glanced at my dad. Why wasn't he saying anything? Usually he was right there with my mom, tag-teaming the discipline. "Yes, your fault."

"How?"

I looked back at my mom. "Don't you get it? You're making me crazy!"

"What?" My mom stood up and leaned over the table, glowering at me like some insane woman. "Do you have any idea what we've gone through to give you opportunities we never had?"

"You?" I jumped up. "I'm the one on scholarship. I'm the one getting straight As. What are you doing?"

"Taking care of your siblings so you can do your homework!"

"You're my mom! That's your job!"

"Frances!" My dad stood up. "Watch it. Your mom works much harder than she should."

"Well, so do I! Do you have any idea how hard I have to work to get my grades? I have a reputation as a loser at school because I never do anything. Then I actually find an activity with other kids that pads my college application as well as gives me a chance to develop social skills, and you have so little trust in me that you won't let me do it? Haven't you noticed that my grades haven't slipped at all, even though I was doing The Homework Club and dating Theo? Don't you get it? I can do it all, and if you refuse to trust me or cut me some slack, you're going to turn me into one of those rebellious drug addicts with pierced nipples who cracked under parental pressure!"

Whew.

My throat hurt after that screaming episode.

But I felt *good*. It was about time I stood up to my parents.

Speaking of parents . . . I eyed Mom and Dad, who were staring at each other with wide eyes and tight lips. What was the look? Shock? Horror? Mental telepathy to grab a straightjacket and haul me off to some institution?

After a moment, my mom sat down.

Then my dad sat down.

"Sit."

I sat, then tucked my hands under my thighs and waited, jiggling my feet under the table. "You need to trust me."

"You lied."

"Because you wouldn't trust me."

My mom sighed, and she didn't look so mad anymore. Deflated, almost, with her sagging shoulders and tight mouth. "We want you to succeed."

"And I am! But I have to have a life, you know. Why can't you give me the freedom until I prove I can't handle it? If my grades slip, then you can reel me in. But as long as I can keep my grades where they are, why can't I have a life too?" I leaned back in my chair. "I was so excited about my success with this story. Everyone was congratulating me all day, even teachers!"

My mom eyed me. "Even teachers?"

"Yes, Mom. Even teachers."

"Huh."

"Imagine what that will do to my college application, to be able to say that as a freshman I was a key figure in changing the administration policy of two schools."

My dad grinned, and even my mom looked thoughtful.

"Think what I could accomplish in the next three years, if you give me the chance."

My mom looked at my dad, who nodded. *Go, Dad!* Mom turned to me. "Frances, you're right. You can do the newspaper next year."

"Really?" Sweet! "There's a meeting tomorrow night. Can I go?" *Please let me go.* I wanted to hear all the comments about my article. Tomorrow night I wouldn't be a loser sitting alone against the wall. Tomorrow night, I'd be in. And then after that, going the next time would be so much easier. I hadn't had the courage to return since that first meeting, but if I could go as the superstar, it would be different. I had to take advantage of it!

"Of course you can," my dad said. "Go. Do it."

I grinned. "And can I go to my friends' houses again?" I saw my mom falter, and I jumped in. "You have to give me a chance to prove myself. I hated lying to you, but I need my friends. Base it on my grades. If they go down, then you can stop me."

My dad nodded, and my mom sort of rolled her eyes. "Fine. But if those grades go down . . ."

"They won't!" I jumped up. I was *so* going over to Blue's house to tell her.

Blue's house.

Which was also Theo's house.

I thought of the night in the backyard, when Theo accused me of not fighting for him.

He was a jerk.

But if I walked out of the kitchen right now without saying anything more, he'd be right.

So I sat back down and clenched my hands in my lap. "What about Theo?"

"No." My mom sat back in her chair. "No dating until you're eighteen."

"Eighteen," my dad repeated.

Non-negotiable. Except I couldn't walk away. "I'm a teenager."

They both eyed me.

"Do you really think you can make me not be interested in boys·for my entire high school career?"

"You can be interested in them, but you can't date them."

I gritted my teeth. "I'm going to date Theo."

"Frances!"

"I'm sick of lying to you guys, so I won't do it anymore. But you have to understand that I'm going to date him. I'd rather have your approval, and that way we would hang out here and you could get to know him and keep an eye on us. But if you refuse to let me, I'll do it anyway." My heart was pounding and my hands were shaking. It was one thing to ask my parents to let me be on the newspaper or hang with my friends, but to openly defy them?

It was exhilarating!

And terrifying.

Because Theo was at stake.

My dad was eyeing me, and again, it really looked like pride in his eyes. "Since when did you grow up?"

I blinked. "What?"

"You're not a kid anymore, are you?"

"No."

He nodded. "You're doing well, Frances. Good job on the article."

I grinned. "Thanks."

My mom cleared her throat. "You aren't thinking of letting her date, are you?"

Dad shook his head. "No."

Oh.

"But it looks to me like she's going to hang out with Theo. I'd rather have her hanging out here where I can watch them. It's not dating, though." He shook his head at me. "No dating."

A glimmer of hope flickered inside me. "No dating," I agreed.

My mom sighed. "No dating."

"And if you're at Blue's house and he's there too, their parents have to be home."

"Agreed." But it would hardly be my fault if I went over there to see Blue and discovered her parents *weren't* home but Theo *was*.

I grinned. Okay, so I wasn't the perfect Frances I used to be. It was a good compromise.

"So, can I go?"

"Where?"

"To Blue's house. To tell her about the article."

My dad narrowed his eyes. "Is Theo going to be there?"

"I have no idea." I hoped so. Unless it was too late for us. I stood up. "I have to go."

"Is your homework done?"

"Not yet, but I'll do it over there." I grabbed my book bag.

"Frances!"

I stopped and looked at my parents. "My homework will be done. I swear."

After a long moment, my dad looked at his watch. "I want you home by eight."

Eight? That was a little early.

Then again, it was better than being grounded.

"Fine. Eight."

He nodded.

I nodded.

Small steps, but huge progress.

One more hurdle to go, and his name was Theo.

I ran out the front door and down the steps, and had just turned right when a voice stopped me.

"Frances."

I spun around. There was Theo, leaning against his car, which was parked in front of my house. He looked *so* good, with his black jeans, his hair blowing in the breeze, his arms folded as if he didn't care about anything.

"Hi," I said, keeping my voice distant.

"Heard about the article."

"You did?"

"Good job."

I grinned. "Thanks. Did you see your name in the article?"

"Yeah. You didn't need to do that."

"I couldn't have done it without you."

He shifted. "You didn't make me sound like a jerk. Left out the first meeting I went to."

"Yeah, well, you redeemed yourself." I took a few steps toward him, stopping just out of his reach. "Why'd you come over here today?"

"To tell you good job." His eyes were wary, his face hard. Sort of how I felt. We hadn't exactly parted on good terms.

"So, I'm not grounded anymore."

He nodded. "Good."

"I can do the paper and hang with my friends."

He lifted a brow.

"No dating, though."

He shrugged. "I don't care."

I took a deep breath. *Just say it, Frances.* "I asked them about you."

His eyes softened for one second and his lips twitched in surprise. "You did?"

"Uh huh. They said I couldn't date you."

"Not a surprise."

"I told them I'd do it anyway."

He didn't say anything. Just looked at me, but the wariness was gone from his face, replaced by a softness that made my heart speed up. "And what did they say?"

"They agreed you could hang out with me at the house. But no dating." I grinned nervously. "I think it's a good start."

He nodded, and didn't say anything. Didn't reach out for me.

Not that I cared.

"About The Homework Club," he said.

"What about it?"

"I kept it going."

Really? "Why?"

"Because you started it. And it was a good thing."

I smiled. "You did it for me?"

He scowled. "No."

"Yes, you did."

"I didn't."

I dropped my backpack on the sidewalk and walked over to him. "You did it for me."

He set his hands on my hips and pulled me against him. "I'd never do anything for a girl."

"Liar."

He grinned.

And then he kissed me.

166

"Frances Spinelli!" My mom hollered from the front porch.

Theo cursed under his breath and pushed me away from him, and I grimaced. Sunk, already? This totally sucked.

"Frances!"

I sighed and turned toward the porch. "What?"

"Don't you and Theo need to come inside the house to do homework?"

"She's not sending me home?" Theo whispered.

Yes. I tried to look smug. "I told you I fought for you."

He looked impressed. "I guess."

"Inside. Homework. Both of you. Now!" My mom stood on the porch and waited.

I picked up my backpack and looked at Theo. "So? Can you take it?"

"Take what?"

"Hanging with a girl who can't go clubbing every night?"

He grinned and grabbed his own bag from his backseat. "I think I can manage."

I smiled and started walking toward the house, only to have Theo catch my arm. "Frances?"

"What?"

"The Homework Club thing? When I kept it going?"

"Yeah?"

"It might have been for you."

I smiled. "I know."

He grinned, and I knew it wouldn't be too long before I found a way to go out dancing with him again. Because he'd turned me into a new person who I was beginning to like very much.

For a jerk, Theo was turning out to be quite the guy.

It's Allie's turn in

WHO NEEDS BOYS?

by Stephie Davis

Coming in July 2005!

CHAPTER ONE

I was heavily immersed in my fantasy about beautiful beaches, endless ocean and oodles of tanned, hot men when my friend Frances elbowed me with a shot of ugly reality.

Latin class.

Ugh.

I pulled out a piece of paper and a pen and jotted her a note. "Why'd you do that? I was fantasizing about Los Angeles. Less than a month away."

She wrote back, "Listen to Mr. Novak."

Well, that was sure fun. Frances and I didn't have the same attitudes toward school, homework and teachers. She studied. I didn't. She listened to teachers. I daydreamed. Why should I take school seriously? It wasn't as if it would make a difference, and who cared what I did anyway? No one. So I did what I wanted.

"Allie? Are you with us?"

I smiled at my teacher. Yeah, sure, he was cute for an old guy but he was still my teacher. "Of course."

"Good." He turned back to the board and finished writing an e-mail address. "During the summer, I run a farm stand. I grow most of my own produce in the fields behind the stand. I need kids to work for me this summer. If any of you are interested, e-mail me."

I raised my hand. "Are we the only people you're asking?" This sounded like a social opportunity if there were boys present. "Or will there be boys there?" Might as well lay it out there. It wasn't as if everyone didn't already know why I was asking.

Mr. Novak folded his arms across his chest and gave me the Look. You know, the one where the teacher is wondering what in the world they're going to do with you. I get it a lot. "Actually, there will be quite a few boys working there as well."

A giggle zipped through the room. I go to an all-girls school, and it's hard to meet boys unless you take initiative. Like me. I initiate a lot and I have plenty of boys in my life.

I'm not about to sit around waiting for them to track me down, because they won't. It's a fact of life. It's not that I'm particularly ugly or anything, it's just that boys don't approach girls, at least not with the frequency I want.

So I take charge.

That's what I'm all about. Taking charge. Being independent. It's not like I want to be like that, but I have no choice. My life would suck if I let it.

"Although there will be boys present, this is not a social opportunity." Mr. Novak appeared to be addressing the class, but he was looking right at me. "It's hard work and I expect full commitment. Anything less and I'll have to let you go. I have a business to run and I need committed people." He nodded to the class. "That's it. Let me know."

Yeesh. He needed to chill. It wasn't as if I was going to actually sign up and ruin his business. I had bigger plans for this summer.

"You want to do it?" Frances asked.

I packed up my notebook. "I can't. I'm going to L.A. for the summer to visit my dad, remember?" I was so psyched. I hadn't been to see him since he'd divorced my mom six years ago, but he was engaged to some woman now and he wanted me to get to know her. Los Angeles in the summer. How cool would that be? Wonder what movie stars I'd see. Maybe I'd get discovered and become a famous actress and never have to come back.

Frances frowned. "For the whole summer? I thought it was only a couple weeks."

I fell into step with her. "The whole summer. Isn't that cool? I'm going to spend the summer at the beach."

She lifted her brow. "Sounds productive."

I rolled my eyes. "Lighten up, Frances. You're productive enough for both of us." And she was. Frances was on full scholarship at our school, and she got straight As. Her parents had staked the family's future on making sure Frances was the first member of the family to go to college. She took the responsibility seriously. Too seriously. Which meant it was up to me to have enough fun for both of us, since she was certainly doing two persons' worth of work.

"I'm going to do it," Frances announced.

"Why? You already have a boyfriend. You don't need to meet boys." Still couldn't believe studious Frances and bad boy Theo were dating. She'd mellowed him, and he'd gotten her to loosen up a little. Not a lot, but a little. They'd never last when he went to college in the fall, but that was okay. Then I'd have her back and I wouldn't have to share her anymore.

"I need the money."

"Oh." Stupid, Allie. I should have realized that. Money was always short at her house. "Then it's a good idea. You should do it."

She nodded. "I wonder if Natalie and Blue want to do it with me."

Natalie and Blue? So the three of them could have some majorly fun adventure this summer at the farm stand without me? I'd come back in September and they'd have all sorts of private jokes that I wouldn't be a part of? "Um . . . I doubt they'll want to do it. Blue will be hanging out with Colin and Natalie probably has running camp or something."

Frances shot me a look. "What's your problem?"

"I don't have a problem. What's yours?"

"You. You're my problem. Why are you being weird? Natalie and Blue will totally go for it and we'll have fun. Maybe we'll even get Natalie a boyfriend so she can double with me and Blue."

While I'm out in L.A. with my dad and his new woman. Alone. Missing out.

I lifted my chin. No, this was fine. I was going to have a great summer. So there. It wouldn't matter that I'd miss out on their fun. I'd create my own and it would be way better.

Besides, I'd be with my dad. Nothing could top that.

We met Natalie and Blue at three o'clock at the town common. It was a huge grassy area flanked by some trees. On sunny, warm days, it was always pretty crowded with people enjoying the weather. Natalie and Blue already had towels out and were cranking tunes. The sun was out and it was a totally awesome June day. Summer was on its way.

I flopped down next to Natalie and helped myself to a chocolate-chip cookie, courtesy of Natalie's mom. Blue's offerings would end up in the trash. Her mom's health food recipes weren't exactly yummy. "Can you believe school is almost out?"

"Less than three weeks," Natalie said. "I'm so excited." She was lying on her back wearing a tank top and shorts. "I can't wait for track to be over. I want to hang out and relax." She opened one eye. "I told my coach I was having female pain, which is why I'm not at practice today."

I grinned. "Way to go, Nat! I'm impressed."

"Was I going to miss out on enjoying this gorgeous afternoon? I couldn't bear to spend it sweating and getting dirty. I can run later, when it's dark." Natalie closed her eyes and held out her hands. "Sun, bake me, please."

"This is our last week of school," I said. The private schools got out way earlier than the public ones. "You guys still have three weeks left?"

"Don't you guys ever have to be in class?" Natalie grumbled.

"At least you have boys around," I said, stretching out beside her. How good did that warm sun feel? Heaven. I couldn't wait for L.A. "I'd trade a short school year for boys in the class in a heartbeat."

"What good does the presence of boys do me? They only think of me as a friend. I'm one of the guys." It was Natalie's ongoing lament. As a runner, she was on coed teams all year long, but it hadn't done anything to help her social life. Which was okay with me. Now that Frances and Blue had boyfriends, Natalie and I had to support each other on Friday nights.

"I might have a solution to your boyfriend situation," Frances said.

I bit my lower lip and tried not to feel jealous, because I knew what Frances was about to offer.

"One of our teachers is hiring kids to work at a farm stand this summer," Frances said. "There will be boys and we earn money."

Natalie sat up. "Really?"

Frances nodded. "I'm going to sign up. Want to do it with me?"

"Yes!"

I frowned. "What about running camp? Aren't you going to running camp this summer?"

Natalie rubbed her chin. "Yeah, but only for a week in August." She looked at Frances. "Do you think he'd let me take off for a week to go to camp?"

"Definitely. He's totally cool."

I tried to imagine some hot, tanned guy rubbing sunscreen onto my back on an endless white beach. That would be so much better than hanging with my friends hauling dirt piles around, right? Of course, right.

"I'm in," Blue said. "Sounds like fun."

I scrunched my eyes shut and thought about meeting Ashton Kutcher on the street and him asking me out. See? I wouldn't miss out by being away from my friends.

"Are you working at the farm stand too, Allie?" Blue asked.

I opened my eyes and put a big smile on my face. "I'm going to L.A. to visit my dad." How cool did that sound when I said it out loud? Yes, I had a dad who wanted to see me.

"I forgot." Blue sighed. "That's so awesome. I wish I was going with you."

"Me too," Natalie said.

By the time my friends finished discussing why L.A. was going to be so awesome and how they were so bummed they couldn't go, I was feeling much better. Yeah, so they'd have a good time this summer without me. I'd have a good time too, and who knew? Maybe my dad would even ask me to live there with him. Maybe this was the first step to him wanting his daughter back in his life.

This was going to be the summer that changed my life. I was certain of it.

Three weeks later, I stood back and eyed all the stacks of clothes on my bed. No way were those going to fit in my two suitcases. Wondered if my mom had another one I could borrow. It was too late to go to the store and buy another one.

The advantage of having an absentee mom who was too busy dating to waste time on her daughter: the Guilt Credit Card. She figured she could buy my loyalty, and who was I to argue? She'd done well in the divorce, so I might as well have some benefit of the nightmare, don't you think? Of course, the credit card only worked when I could use it. At ten o'clock on Friday night, there was nowhere I was going to find a suitcase for sale.

I stuck my head out into the hall. "Mom? Are you here?"

Silence.

The disadvantage of having an absentee mom: she was never around.

I frowned as I wandered into her room to check under the bed for another suitcase. Should I call a cab for the airport tomorrow? She'd sworn she would take me, but she'd forgotten before. She'd even been squeezed out of the carpool circle with my friends.

After my mom left us at the movie theater at midnight, Blue's mom had decided that she'd take over my mom's duties.

Which was fine. Got us home, didn't it? And I had learned not to care that she wasn't home or didn't seem to give a rip if my head fell off and rolled out into the street. She'd just step over my beheaded body on her way out to her next date. Exactly how I liked it. I didn't need her. Which is why I was going to do everything in my power to convince my dad to invite me to stay out in L.A. with him. Yeah, sure, I'd miss my friends, but by the end of the summer I'd be dating Justin Timberlake and all his friends would be mine, and I'd have no room for missing my friends.

But first, I had to get all my cute clothes out to California with me, and that wasn't going to happen with my two small suitcases.

I dropped to my knees and peered under my mom's bed.

Nothing under the bed except dust and a pair of Ferragamos she'd discarded. Completely unfortunate that her feet were two sizes bigger than mine.

I checked her closet. Nothing. Time to try my sister's room.

Rifled through, but of course she'd taken her luggage with her when she'd gone off to London for a summer program to get her a step ahead before starting college in the fall. She had left behind a sweet black miniskirt and a lace camisole I'd been coveting for ages. Now they were mine!

Excellent. Wish I had time to spend more hours in there searching for lost treasures Louisa had left behind. I sighed as I walked out of her room clutching my new clothes. I really missed her. Yeah, she'd been out with her friends a lot over the last year, but she was around to give me advice about boys or makeup or my friends.

And now she was in London getting educated. Or at least, that's what she'd said to my mom. I knew it was because she wanted to get out of there, just like I did.

I stood in the upstairs hall and listened to the utter silence of the house. And to think I'd been upset I was missing out with my friends this summer. No way was hanging out with them worth enduring this tomb for three months, not when I had the option of going to L.A. with my dad.

Speaking of which, I really needed to find a duffel bag or something.

The front hall closet held nothing, and neither did the guest room. Darn it! There had to be something somewhere.

I walked to the kitchen and dialed my mom. I wasn't supposed to bother her on dates unless it was an emergency, but this definitely constituted an emergency, don't you think? Besides, she'd probably forgotten this was my last night at home and she'd appreciate the reminder so she could rush home and spend some quality time with me before I took off.

The phone rang and then went into voicemail.

So I dialed again. Same result. "Mom, call me as soon as you can."

Guess I was on my own to pack.

I kicked at the steps as I stomped back upstairs. Shouldn't someone want to see me off tonight? Shouldn't my mom be sad her daughter was leaving for three months? You'd think one night off from the dating scene wouldn't have killed her.

The doorbell rang before I made it to the top. "Mom?" Grinning, I ran down the stairs and flung it open. It was Natalie, Blue and Frances, their boyfriends, and pizza and soda and DVDs. Not as good as my mom, but also better than her. "What are you guys doing here?"

"Farewell party for Allie of course," Natalie announced. "You didn't think we were going to forget, did you?"

I couldn't wipe the grin off my face. "Maybe I did, a little." This was awesome! My true friends.

"Loser." Blue hugged me and then led the way inside. "To the family room," she announced. "That's where the surround sound is."

Theo, who was both Blue's older brother and Frances's boyfriend, slung his arm over my shoulder and hauled me into the living room. "You know we'll miss you."

I've known Theo since I was a baby. We'd all known each other forever, except for Colin, of course, Blue's boyfriend. But Colin was totally cool and fit in like he'd been one of the crew forever.

I was going to miss them. A lot. What if my dad didn't love me? What if I got out to L.A. and it was horrible?

"What's wrong?" Natalie slid next to me on the couch.

"Nothing." I looked around. "Where are the boys for me and Natalie?" I still hadn't figured out why Colin and Theo didn't bring their friends around for Natalie and I to try on for size. Probably because their friends were too cool to hang with a bunch of freshman girls. Well, forget that. I wasn't a freshman anymore. School was out, and I was on my way to being a sophomore. Totally worthy of older boys. No, not boys. Guys. Men. Hot, sexy men who were waiting for me in L.A.

Colin grinned. "There were so many guys who wanted to come that we couldn't decide, so we decided not to bring anyone. But you girls were highly sought after."

"Yeah, right." I rolled my eyes and flopped back on the couch. "I'll have plenty of my own boys when I get to L.A." Then I sat up. "No, not boys. Men. I'll have men."

"You're only fourteen," Natalie pointed out. She was the only one who could talk about the age differential, since Blue and Frances were both dating older guys.

"Fifteen in a month. And I look like I'm eighteen." I shot a look at the boys. "Don't I?"

They exchanged wary glances, and I laughed. As if they'd go there with their girlfriends sitting next to them. Boys were so transparent. That's why I needed a man. A tanned, California man.

Frances held up a DVD. "We got *The Sure Thing*. It's old, but it's about how much better California is than the ucky Northeast, so we figured it would be good."

"Cool." I helped myself to a piece of pizza and tried not to be sad that I'd miss them. It was only for the summer. We'd be back together in the fall. Unless my dad asked me to stay. Right now, I almost didn't want to leave them. I mean, my friends were the only people in my life who would notice if I disappeared off the earth. Not only would they notice, but they'd care and actually try to find me. But maybe my dad was ready for that. He had invited me out for the whole summer, hadn't he? I sighed. Still didn't make it easier to leave my friends. "You guys won't, um, forget about me while I'm gone will you?"

"No!" Blue flung her arms around me, and Natalie and Frances followed suit until I was being squashed underneath the pile. I screamed and hugged them back. And tickled them until we were all screaming.

Somewhere between the elbows, I heard the phone ring.

"Someone get that. It's probably my mom calling back." As if I could get it. I was totally being pig-piled.

Then Theo interrupted the love fest. "It's your dad."

"My dad!" I scrambled free and grabbed the phone. "Dad?"

"How are you doing, hon?"

I walked into the living room and snuggled up on the couch. "I'm great. I'm almost finished packing. I can't wait." It was so good to hear his voice. I couldn't believe how long it had been since I'd seen him.

"Um . . . Allie . . ."

Something caught in my throat. "What's wrong?"

"Nothing's wrong. It's fine."

"What's fine?" I tucked my feet under a pillow and tried to keep my voice calm.

"It's Heidi."

"Your fiancée?" I thought of the gorgeous brunette my dad had e-mailed me a picture of last week. She looked way younger than my dad, but didn't everyone in California look young and beautiful?

"Yes. She's . . . ah . . . pregnant."

"Pregnant? I'm going to have a little sister or brother?" Oh my gosh. That was so cool. A fresh start at a family. Yes! They'd totally need my help now! "You want me to be a nanny? I can totally do that. I'll watch her or him after school and . . ."

"Allie, hon, calm down."

"But this is cool! I can't wait to get out there. Will the baby be born this summer?"

"No, not until winter, but Heidi is really sick. The pregnancy isn't going well."

I frowned. "How sick?"

"Very sick. She's . . . ah . . . I don't think it would be a good idea for you to come out this summer."

My gut plummeted. "What?"

"I am going to have to take care of her, and she's on bed rest. Neither of us can be worrying about you."

I swallowed hard. "But I'm very independent. You don't have to worry about me at all. I can cook. I'll be your housekeeper. I'll take care of her while you're at work."

"I'm sorry, Allie. It will be too stressful. If things change, we'll call. Otherwise, can we take a rain check for next summer?"

"A rain check?" *A rain check?* "But I'm really easy. You won't even notice I'm there." I couldn't keep the tears out of my voice. "Dad?"

"I'm sorry, hon. It's just not the right time. I love you, and I'll call you in a couple days. I have to run. Bye."

I sat there with the phone buzzing in my ear. I couldn't believe it.

No, I could believe it. I should have predicted it. How could I have been so stupid as to get my hopes up? After six years of excuses, you'd have thought I would have been smarter than that.

"Allie? You okay?" Frances was standing in the doorway, her face all scrunched up in concern.

I tossed the phone on the couch and smiled at her. "I have great news!"

"What?"

"I don't have to go to L.A.! I'm going to hang with you guys this summer. Isn't that great?" It was great. No way was I going to let my dad ruin my summer. Forget him. And next summer if he asked me back? *I'd* bail on *him* at the last second. Hah.

Frances frowned. "I thought you wanted to go to L.A."

"I was talking myself into it because I had to go. You know I was bummed to miss out on the farm stand thing." I swallowed hard and kept a grin on my face. "This will be great."

"But Mr. Novak said his staff was full. That there was no room."

For an instant, I felt my smile slip. What if I was stuck at home all summer? In this horrible, empty house with no air-conditioning? Then I recovered. Mr. Novak was male. I could talk males into anything.

Except my dad apparently, but he wasn't male. He was a jerk.

"I'll call him." I headed for the kitchen and the phone book, delighted to find only three Sam Novaks. "There. I'll call each of them."

Frances's eyes were wide. "You're going to call him at home?"

"Of course. This is a crisis. I can't miss out on summer with you guys." And because if I had to spend the entire summer alone I knew I would totally freak out. I decided to start at the bottom. A woman answered. "Is the Mr. Novak who lives there the one who teaches Latin?"

"Yes, it is. Who is this?"

I gave Frances the thumbs up. "One of his students. Can I talk to him?"

"He's not here. Can I take a message?"

Oh, wow. I hadn't thought of that. "Um . . . yeah . . . I was calling about the farm stand. I wanted to work for him."

"Sorry, sweetie, but it's full. You're the seventh person who has called him today, but there's no more space."

"But . . . " I was horrified by the tears that sprung to my eyes. I immediately spun around so Frances couldn't see. "You don't understand. All my friends are doing it."

"Then you should have signed up with them." Her voice was gentle, but unyielding.

"But I couldn't." I swallowed to crush the emotion rising in my throat. "I was supposed to go see my dad and he cancelled on me five minutes ago even though I haven't seen him for six years and he has this fiancée and I can't go and my mom's never home and I don't want to be alone all summer and . . ." I realized I was sobbing now, and I immediately shut my mouth.

Well, except for when I had to open it to suck in air. Heaving sobs were not the most dignified.

"What's your name?" The woman's voice was sympathetic and it made me want to start crying again. I hated sympathy. I was fine. Totally fine.

"Allie Morrison."

"What's your phone number?"

I gave it to her.

"I'll talk to Sam when he gets home, okay?"

"I have to be able to work there. I'll even do it for free. I'll do anything. I just can't stay here." How desperate did I sound? I never begged. Ever.

"He'll call you, but it might not be until tomorrow."

"Okay. I'll wait by the phone." I hung up and turned around. All my friends plus Colin and Theo were standing in the kitchen watching me.

I immediately wiped the tears off my cheeks and raised my chin. "I think we need to put in a different movie, don't you? I'm not feeling in a pro-California mood anymore."

Without waiting for a response, I grabbed a gallon of ice cream from the freezer, a spoon and marched into the family room.

Mr. Novak better not let me down.

❧ STEPHIE DAVIS ❧

PUTTING BOYS ON THE LEDGE

You like a boy, but he blows you off. You're bummed out. Guess what? You're on The Ledge. It's a rotten place to be, which is why boys belong out there, not girls! Keep boys out on The Ledge and they'll never be able to hurt you.

Why would Blue Waller want to put a gorgeous senior on The Ledge just when he's starting to notice her? But if she doesn't, will he end up breaking her heart?

Blue—that's short for Blueberry—is cursed with the worst name on the planet, parents that seriously hamper her social life, and the figure of her eight-year-old sister. Good thing she has three best friends to help her find true love—even if it means braving The Ledge.

- -

The Year My Life Went Down the Loo
by Katie Maxwell

Subject: The Grotty and the Fabu (No, it's not a song.)
From: Mrs.Oded@btelecom.co.uk
To: Dru@seattlegrrl.com

Things That Really Irk My Pickle About Living in England

- The school uniform
- Piddlington-on-the-weld (I will forever be known as Emily from *Piddlesville*)
- Marmite (It's yeast sludge! GACK!)
- The ghost in my underwear drawer (Spectral hands fondling my bras—enough said!)
- No malls! What are these people *thinking???*

Things That Keep Me From Flying Home to Seattle for Good Coffee

- Aidan (*Hunkalicious!*)
- Devon (*Droolworthy?* Understatement of the year!)
- Fang (He puts the *num* in *nummy!*)
- Holly (Any girl who hunts movie stars with me—and Oded Fehr *will be mine*—is a friend for life.)
- Über-coolio Polo Club (Where the snogging is FINE!)

They Wear WHAT Under Their Kilts?

by Katie Maxwell

Subject: Emily's Glossary for People Who Haven't Been to Scotland
From: Mrs.Legolas@kiltnet.com
To: Dru@seattlegrrl.com

Faffing about: running around doing nothing. In other words, spending a month supposedly doing work experience on a Scottish sheep farm, but really spending days on Kilt Watch at the nearest castle.

Schottie: Scottish Hottie, also known as Ruaraidh.

Mad schnoogles: the British way of saying big smoochy kisses. Will admit it sounds v. smart to say it that way.

Bunch of yobbos: a group of mindless idiots. In Scotland, can also mean sheep.

Stooshie: uproar, as in, "If Holly thinks she can take Ruaraidh from me without causing a stooshie, she's out of her mind!"

Sheep dip: not an appetizer.

What's French For "EW!"?

KATIE MAXWELL

Subject: Emily's Handy Phrases For Spring Break in Paris

From: Em-the-enforcer@englandrocks.com

To: Dru@seattlegrrl.com

J'apprendrais par coeur plutôt le Klingon qu'essaye d'apprendre le français en deux semaines.
I would rather memorize Klingon than try to learn French in two weeks.

Vous voulez que je mange un escargot?
You want me to *EAT* a snail?!?

Vous êtes nummy, mais mon petit ami est le roi des hotties, et il vient à Paris seulement pour me voir!
You are nummy, but my boyfriend is the king of hotties, and he's coming to Paris just to see me!

THE REAL DEAL

Unscripted
Amy Kaye

Thanks to the reality-TV show that records her junior year in excruciating detail, Claire Marangello gets her big break: her own version of the TV show and a starring role in a Broadway musical. Plus Jeb, a way-hot co-star who seems to like her *that* way, and a half sister she didn't know she had. It's everything she's ever dreamed of.

Or is it a total nightmare? Her sister seems to be drifting away. Claire's not sure she can trust Jeb and his weird celebrity-centered world. The director seems to hate her; the dance steps are harder than she'd ever imagined. Claire's about to learn that while being a Broadway star is a challenge, real life has twists and turns harder than any onstage choreography and is totally . . . *UNSCRIPTED*.

Dorchester Publishing Co., Inc.
P.O. Box 6640   ___5315-2
Wayne, PA 19087-8640 $5.99 US/$7.99 CAN

Please add $2.50 for shipping and handling for the first book and $.75 for each additional book.
NY and PA residents, add appropriate sales tax. No cash, stamps, or CODs. Canadian orders
require an extra $2.00 for shipping and handling and must be paid in U.S. dollars. Prices and
availability subject to change. **Payment must accompany all orders.**

Name: _____

Address: _____

City: _____ State: _____ Zip: _____

E-mail: _____

I have enclosed $_____ in payment for the checked book(s).

CHECK OUT OUR WEBSITE! www.smoochya.com
_____ Please send me a free catalog.

Amy Kaye

THE REAL DEAL
Focus on *THIS!*

Caught on tape: The newest reality television series goes on location somewhere truly dangerous—high school. Outrageous and unscripted, each episode exposes the sickest gossip, finds the facts behind the rumors, and bares the raw truth. Tune in and take it all in, because no subject is too taboo, no secret too private, and no behavior off limits!

Meet Fiona O'Hara—stuck in a suburban sitcom a million light-years away from her native New York City, a.k.a. civilization. Her mom is a basket case since the divorce. Her dad is Mr. Disappearo. And the one guy who seems like a decent love-interest has a psycho wannabe girlfriend who's ready to put a hit out on her.

Kaz Delaney ❄
My Life as a Snow Bunny

LERVE: LOVE WITH A SWISS ACCENT

It can:

✔ Warm up the chilly ski slopes.
Who knew Colorado was Hunk Heaven? Not Jo Vincent.

✔ Provide a fun distraction.
It's not like Jo's going to get any attention from her dad. He
brought his own après-ski entertainment—her name is Kate.

✔ Happen with Hans.
Every girl should experience one in her life: a Swiss
guy as smooth as chocolate and just as sweet . . .
So European! So regal! So mysterious! Like . . .
❄ what's all this stuff about kangaroos?

A Girl, A Guy & A Ghost

Sherrie Rose

Traci Nettleton is in seventh heaven when Brad Davidson, the gorgeous quarterback on the football team, asks her out. Then she gets a mysterious e-mail that threatens to ruin everything.

Brad loves hanging out with Traci. She's cute, smart, and funny. But she seems a little jumpy around him lately. Is she hiding something?

How can Traci be getting e-mails from her best friend who died two years ago? Is someone playing a cruel practical joke, or does Corky really need her help? Traci plans to find out—her new romance with Brad depends on it.

Didn't want this book to end?

There's more waiting at **www.smoochya.com**:

Win FREE books and makeup!
Read excerpts from other books!
Chat with the authors!
Horoscopes!
Quizzes!

 Bringing you the books on everyone's lips!